WANTED – A ROYAL WIFE

As Prince Kraus was speaking his eyes suddenly closed and his head fell back against the cushion behind him.

"You are in pain!" cried Latasha without thinking.

"It's this ghastly migraine," he murmured.

Now there was a deep frown on his forehead and he squeezed his eyes as if the pain was almost unbearable.

Latasha rose to her feet. Going behind Prince Kraus's chair, she placed her hands very gently on his forehead.

"Try to relax," she urged. "I am going to massage your forehead gently and I hope it will take away the pain."

She spoke very quietly.

At the same time she started to move her fingers as her mother had shown her over his forehead and down by his temples.

She had seen her mother doing it so often to people who had come to her from the village.

Prince Kraus did not say anything and as Latasha continued to massage his head very very gently, she felt him begin to relax.

He was no longer tense with pain.

She remembered exactly the movements her mother had made on a sufferer's head.

As she used her fingers she prayed as her mother had always done.

THE BARBARA CARTLAND PINK COLLECTION

Titles in this series

WANTED –
A ROYAL WIFE

BARBARA CARTLAND

Barbaracartland.com Ltd

THE BARBARA CARTLAND PINK COLLECTION

Barbara Cartland was the most prolific bestselling author in the history of the world. She was frequently in the Guinness Book of Records for writing more books in a year than any other living author. In fact her most amazing literary feat was when her publishers asked for more Barbara Cartland romances, she doubled her output from 10 books a year to over 20 books a year, when she was 77.

She went on writing continuously at this rate for 20 years and wrote her last book at the age of 97, thus completing 400 books between the ages of 77 and 97.

Her publishers finally could not keep up with this phenomenal output, so at her death she left 160 unpublished manuscripts, something again that no other author has ever achieved.

Now the exciting news is that these 160 original unpublished Barbara Cartland books are already being published and by Barbaracartland.com exclusively on the internet, as the international web is the best possible way of reaching so many Barbara Cartland readers around the world.

The 160 books are published monthly and will be numbered in sequence.

The series is called the Pink Collection as a tribute to Barbara Cartland whose favourite colour was pink and it became very much her trademark over the years.

The Barbara Cartland Pink Collection is published only on the internet. Log on to www.barbaracartland.com to find out how you can purchase the books monthly as they are published, and take out a subscription that will ensure that all subsequent editions are delivered to you by mail order to your home.

NEW

Barbaracartland.com is proud to announce the publication of ten new Audio Books for the first time as CDs. They are favourite Barbara Cartland stories read by well-known actors and actresses and each story extends to 4 or 5 CDs. The Audio Books are as follows:

The Patient Bridegroom	The Passion and the Flower
A Challenge of Hearts	Little White Doves of Love
A Train to Love	The Prince and the Pekinese
The Unbroken Dream	A King in Love
The Cruel Count	A Sign of Love

More Audio Books will be published in the future and the above titles can be purchased by logging on to the website www.barbaracartland.com or please write to the address below.

If you do not have access to a computer, you can write for information about the Barbara Cartland Pink Collection and the Barbara Cartland Audio Books to the following address:

Barbara Cartland.com Ltd., Camfield Place,
Hatfield, Hertfordshire AL9 6JE, United Kingdom.

Telephone: +44 (0)1707 642629
Fax: +44 (0)1707 663041

THE LATE DAME BARBARA CARTLAND

Barbara Cartland who sadly died in May 2000 at the age of nearly 99 was the world's most famous romantic novelist who wrote 723 books in her lifetime with worldwide sales of over 1 billion copies and her books were translated into 36 different languages.

As well as romantic novels, she wrote historical biographies, 6 autobiographies, theatrical plays, books of advice on life, love, vitamins and cookery. She also found time to be a political speaker and television and radio personality.

She wrote her first book at the age of 21 and this was called *Jigsaw*. It became an immediate bestseller and sold 100,000 copies in hardback and was translated into 6 different languages. She wrote continuously throughout her life, writing bestsellers for an astonishing 76 years. Her books have always been immensely popular in the United States, where in 1976 her current books were at numbers 1 & 2 in the B. Dalton bestsellers list, a feat never achieved before or since by any author.

Barbara Cartland became a legend in her own lifetime and will be best remembered for her wonderful romantic novels, so loved by her millions of readers throughout the world.

Her books will always be treasured for their moral message, her pure and innocent heroines, her good looking and dashing heroes and above all her belief that the power of love is more important than anything else in everyone's life.

"Love can appear in so many different and unexpected ways and always when one least expects it, so don't be surprised on a boat, a train or even a bus!"

Barbara Cartland

CHAPTER ONE
1887

Lady Latasha Ling rode into the stable yard.

The Head Groom came hurrying out to her horse's head.

"He is an excellent jumper, Abbey," Lady Latasha said, "and I think when he has had a little more training, he will beat His Grace's favourite, who he continually says is unbeatable."

Abbey laughed.

"That be so very true, my Lady," he replied. "I've great 'opes of this 'ere 'orse, 'e certainly shapes better than any of them other 'orses."

"I agree with you, Abbey, but we will not upset His Grace until we race him and win!"

Latasha walked on to the house, thinking as she did so that it would be such fun to beat her brother's champion horse as Solomon had already won quite a number of races.

The sun was shining and the garden was filled with flowers.

She thought that nothing could be more lovely than Norlington Park in the spring.

She walked into the house through one of the many French windows.

She had lived in the great house, which dated back for four hundred years, ever since she was a child.

1

As she often told herself, she loved every inch of it and she had certainly missed her home when she had gone to a boarding school.

She had returned back home a year ago having won several prizes and with a report that her brother said should be hung in every schoolroom to challenge other pupils to try to equal it.

Walking along the passage towards the hall Latasha wondered if her brother had returned.

He had left early that morning to visit a farm where there had been a fire.

She hoped he would not bring back bad news and that there had not been any great damage.

She reached the hall and was handing her gloves and whip to a footman when the butler announced,

"His Grace has now returned, my Lady, and wishes you to join him in the study at your convenience."

"I hoped he would be, Barnet, and I hope too that he has brought us good news about Estowe Farm."

"I hope the same, my Lady. We've never had any trouble there before."

Barnet had been at Norlington Park for nearly forty years.

He had come first as a scullery-boy, moved up to help in the pantry, then after a number of years as footman had risen to the position of butler.

Like all the elderly servants he thought of the Park as his home. He always spoke as if he was one of the family – which indeed he virtually was.

Latasha walked to the study thinking that if the fire at Estowe Farm had been a very bad one, everyone would be feeling concerned for the farmer and his family.

She opened the study door.

Her brother, as she had expected, was sitting at his writing desk.

He had been the Duke for only two years and took his duties extremely seriously, spending most of his time at home in the country looking after the vast estate.

He did however hold a hereditary position at Court.

Queen Victoria liked having young and handsome gentlemen around her.

He had therefore to turn up at Windsor Castle more often than he really wished to do.

As his sister came into the room, he looked up and smiled.

He was a good-looking young man, just as Latasha was a beauty.

She had been acclaimed last year when she was a *debutante* and all the Society newspapers always wrote in glowingly complimentary terms about her.

"You are now back, Latasha!" the Duke exclaimed unnecessarily as she walked towards him. "How did the new horse behave?"

"He is magnificent, Harry. In fact I think that he is going to be better than all the rest put together."

"High praise indeed. I only hope you are right. He cost a lot of money and I am glad to hear you think he is worth it."

"He is certainly worth at least double or treble what you gave for him. Now tell me about Estowe farm. Was the fire very bad?"

"Fortunately the fire did not touch the farmhouse itself. There are two barns which will need a great deal of repair or rebuilding. Otherwise we escaped lightly."

"I am so glad. Is that what you wanted to tell me?"

"That and something else, which you will doubtless think is more important – "

She raised her eyebrows and sank down into a chair next to his writing desk.

"Tell me what it is."

"It's a letter from Kraus."

He thought his sister looked vague.

"You know just who I mean – His Royal Highness Prince Kraus of Oldessa."

"Oh, of course, Harry, now I do know who you are talking about. For a moment I could not place the name."

The Duke picked up a letter from his writing desk.

He stared at it without speaking and after a moment Latasha enquired,

"What is in the letter. What does he say and what is upsetting you?"

"It is not exactly upsetting me, Latasha. But it is a surprise I had not expected".

Latasha did not say anything.

She knew of old that her brother was inclined to be hesitant in coming to the point when there was anything of importance to say.

"I think," he said eventually, "that I had better read you the whole letter."

"Yes, do," murmured Latasha.

The Duke began,

"*My dear Harry,*

I often think of you and the fun we had when we were at Oxford together.

I have always been hoping that you would make an effort to come out and stay with me now that I have become the Ruler of Oldessa.

But things have been somewhat upsetting last year as of course you are well aware.

I was very fond of Alexander and it is so appalling what happened to him. As you can well understand all the small Principalities like my own are afraid that the same misfortune may happen to them.

The only way we can save ourselves is to have the support and protection of Great Britain."

The Duke paused for breath and Latasha knew just what he was talking about.

Everyone in Europe had been horrified the previous year when the Russians under their Czar Alexander III had contrived in a most disgraceful way to take over Bulgaria which was ruled by Prince Alexander of Battenburg.

Many Balkan Princes had been too weak to stand up to persistent Russian infiltration and they had become nothing more than Russian puppets.

Prince Alexander however refused to submit to the Russian's demands, but the Czar was determined to have his own way.

Russian agents stirred up a mutiny in the Bulgarian Army, kidnapped Prince Alexander and then forced him to abdicate at pistol point.

He was taken by ship and deposited in the Russian port of Reni.

Latasha could remember the outcry in England and in every other European country.

Queen Victoria raged that the Russians' behaviour was appalling and 'without parallel in modern history.' In fact she was so angry that Czar Alexander was forced very soon to return the Prince to Bulgaria.

Prince Alexander was, however, as all his friends knew, deeply disillusioned by the treachery of his Army, so he surrendered his throne and retired to a quiet private life.

Latasha secretly believed at the time that it would have been braver of Prince Alexander to continue to reign, especially as the Czar had been compelled to give way on his account.

However, she was not all that interested, but merely distrusted the Russians even more than previously.

Her brother was now continuing to read the letter,

"My Prime Minister and my Secretary of State for Foreign Affairs persist in begging me to approach Queen Victoria and ask Her Majesty, as so many Balkan Princes have already done, to provide me with an English bride.

I appreciate only too well what this would mean to Oldessa. But as I am not at all well, I have no intention of marrying at the moment and may never do so in the future.

However, what I do believe is desirable is that my brother Stefan – who is the heir presumptive as I have no children – should have the enormous advantage of being protected by the British. And that is why, Harry, as an old friend, I am asking you for your help."

The Duke paused again.

He looked a little apprehensively at his sister.

As she did not speak, he resumed reading,

"I know your sister, Lady Latasha, is now grown up and I remember how pretty you told me she was as a child.

If she would consider marrying Stefan and in a few years, perhaps sooner, rule Oldessa with him, it would be a tremendous benefit from our point of view.

As your sister's Guardian you will understand what pleasure and happiness it would give to me."

As he finished the sentence, the Duke looked up.

His sister was staring at him with an expression of sheer astonishment.

"Is he," she asked, "actually asking me to go and marry his brother whom I have never met or even heard of until now?"

"I met him, Latasha, some years ago. He is a very good-looking and charming young man and from what I have heard is a great success with the ladies."

"*Hardly* a recommendation as a husband," Latasha retorted sharply.

"Well you certainly would not want a man who was so unattractive that no one would look at him! Seriously, Latasha, I think you should consider this suggestion."

He saw that his sister was about to speak and went on quickly,

"I know a good deal about Oldessa and it is a most delightful country. Not very large, if you compare it with its neighbours, Hungary and Bulgaria. But it breeds horses which can beat those of Hungary and has Steppes to ride on."

Latasha appeared a little more interested.

"It is, from everything Kraus has always told me, extremely beautiful and the people themselves are friendly, peaceful and remarkably intelligent."

"You make it sound just like a fairyland," Latasha countered scornfully. "But I am extremely happy here in England and that is where I wish to stay."

Her brother held up the letter.

"I think I should read you the next few lines – "

"I am listening, Harry."

"Kraus says further – "

"*We are all aware here that Queen Victoria, who is known as the 'Matchmaker of Europe', has been providing British Royal brides as a major defence against the Czar's ambition to take over the whole of the Balkans.*

I am therefore half afraid that your sister may well already be spoken for, since I know that your mother was a distant relative of Her Majesty. If this is so, I shall be very angry with myself for not having written to you sooner.

If by a fortunate chance your sister is still available, please can you persuade her that we would do everything in our power to make her happy.

I would love her, not just because she is your sister, but because she would save my country from the greedy ambitions of the Russian Czar."

Listening, Latasha knew this was in fact true.

Queen Victoria had supplied an astounding number of relatives as Consorts to European rulers.

She could quite understand that Oldessa desired the protection of Britain and the best way to be sure of it was to have a Queen on their throne who was British.

The Duke had heard many speeches on the subject in the House of Lords and had discussed with Members of the Cabinet what could be done about the situation in the Balkans.

Bismarck had set out to unite the smaller German Principalities into one large Empire and his great success had made Czar Alexander III think that if Prussia could do so, well, Russia could do even better.

He was furious that Russia had failed in what he thought was her mission to dominate the Balkans and win control of the Dardanelles and thus give the Russian fleet full access to the Mediterranean.

Stubbornly the Czar was determined to win what he desired by more subtle means.

He would not under any circumstances go openly to war, but he would gain his ends by surreptitious methods which would not be recognised until it was too late to fight back against them.

Although the Duke was well aware how serious the situation was, he had never imagined for one moment that he or his family might be personally involved.

In addition the Marquis of Salisbury had just been appointed Secretary of State for Foreign Affairs.

Since he was well acquainted with the Duke and his family, an offer which was more or less a command might come at any moment.

As if she could read her brother's thoughts, Latasha asked,

"If it happened to me, would I be able to refuse?"

"It would be most difficult for you to do so. You know what the Queen is like when she gets an idea in her head. She expects to be obeyed 'at the double'."

Latasha did not even smile and he continued,

"I have a feeling that by the time you realised what was happening, you would be married and sitting on the throne of Oldessa."

"How can I marry a man of whom I know nothing and you know very little too? You have only seen him as a boy."

"I would much rather you married my friend Kraus. He is a charming and very brave man. He was wounded in a nasty skirmish with some Russians who had, of course, caused trouble. He had insisted on removing the intruders himself rather than leaving them to his Army Officers."

"But if he is the same age as you, Harry, and you are not yet twenty-eight, surely he will recover?"

"I suppose he knows better than us what is wrong," the Duke replied, "but he has a brother who could succeed to the throne."

There was silence and then the Duke remarked,

"I have not finished the letter. You had better hear it all."

Latasha did not answer and he read on,

"I have another rather different request and here I would be extremely grateful if you could help me as soon as possible.

My sister, Amalie, who I do not think you have met, is now sixteen.

I am very anxious for her to speak English fluently. As you know it has always been a great help to me that I was educated at Oxford University with you.

The only Governesses who can speak in English in this part of the world are old, dull and not always reliable.

If you can send me out an English Governess who is young and could be a charming companion as well as a teacher for Amalie, I think besides improving her English, it would make her much happier than she is at the moment.

This is all a cry for help!

Please help me, Harry, out of the kindness of your heart which has never failed me in the past.

I do not want to sound morbid, but unless I receive help, the menacing hand of Russia may easily fall upon me and my beloved country."

The Duke put down the letter on his desk.

"I have had many requests for help in my time," he reflected, "but this is the most demanding and the most difficult."

"You are so right," agreed Latasha. "Insofar as it concerns me, I would love to tear up that letter, run away, and hide in a cave where no one can find me!"

"I can easily understand your feelings, but equally you cannot remain in a cave for the rest of your life. Now I think about it, I am worried that I might be summoned to Windsor Castle at any moment.

"Someone was only saying the other day that Her Majesty was finding it almost impossible to assist all the Balkan Princes who are constantly beseeching her to send them a Consort."

He gave a laugh which had no humour in it, as he added,

"I am told that one reigning Prince who requested an English bride is nearly eighty and both blind and deaf!"

"Apparently Prince Stefan is not quite as bad as all that," murmured Latasha. "But I cannot agree to marry a man I have never seen and whom I do not know."

"I was just thinking, Latasha, if we both went out there for a visit, would that make things any better?"

"It would make it much worse. How could we stay with them and then at the end of the visit say I do not like him and am unwilling to marry him!"

She threw up her hands.

"You know perfectly well I would be unable to say so since you and Prince Kraus are such good friends."

"I do see difficulties about it," the Duke admitted. "But are there any of our relations who would like to be the reigning Princess of the petty Principality?"

"I was just thinking the same. All I can think of at the moment are the aunts who are getting on for sixty and our cousins most of whom are still in a perambulator!"

The Duke laughed.

"That is just the sort of joke Her Majesty would not think funny!"

"I do not think it funny that I might have to go out to this tiresome Principality and find my bridegroom is so unpleasant that I cannot bear to look at him."

"Now you are exaggerating, Latasha."

"Have you forgotten, Harry, that we have a perfect example of one such marriage in Helen?"

There was no need for her to say any more.

Helen was their elder sister who had been born two years before Harry.

When she was eighteen she was very lovely and she made quite a stir in the Social world when she appeared as a *debutante*.

The Ruler of a small Principality in the South of Germany had met her and he realised that she was not only exceedingly attractive but also had Royal breeding.

There was no doubt Helen's antecedents were the envy of a great number of Germans of lesser consequence.

It had all seemed very glamorous and exciting and the Prince himself was a tall good-looking young man.

Helen accepted his proposal of marriage.

It was only two years ago that Latasha had realised how unhappy she was.

On Helen's last visit to England, she had wailed,

"I now cannot bear to go back to Germany. If only I could stay with you and Harry."

"Are you *really* unhappy, Helen?" asked Latasha.

As there were many years between the two sisters, they did not often communicate with each other and Helen had never been confidential with Latasha.

She had hesitated before she explained,

"I cannot describe to you the utter boredom of it. I see nothing but women – old fat German women who have never had a thought in their heads that is not domestic and dull."

"But you have your husband," Latasha pointed out wonderingly.

"Otto is very polite to me in public and he gives me

anything I require. But in the last three or four years he has taken on a number of mistresses."

Latasha stared at her sister in astonishment.

"*Mistresses*!" she exclaimed.

"Of course," replied Helen. "He finds a wife dull, and as I have given him two sons and a daughter he has no more need to be particularly interested in me as when we first married."

"Oh, Helen, I am *so* sorry. It never occurred to me you were unhappy."

"*Bored* is the right word," replied her sister. "I am *bored* with the Germans, their conversation, their food and their passion for noisy music. If only I could come home for a year or so, I would begin to think it was worth going on living."

"Oh, Helen, why not do so?" enquired Latasha.

"There would be a great commotion if I did. Of course as the Prince's wife I sit on numerous committees, I receive deputations from women, I visit schools and talk to fat little German children who are much happier that I am. But there is nothing to make my heart feel as if it is leaping with joy as it used to before I married."

Latasha was very upset at what Helen had said, but there was nothing she could do about it.

Soon Helen would have to leave for Germany as a letter from her husband told her that they had an important engagement at which they had to receive the Emperor.

She departed without saying anything further.

As Latasha waved her goodbye she felt that Helen's beauty, which was very English and at the same time very classical, was wasted on all those Germans – they did not appreciate either her beauty or her brains.

When she told Harry what Helen had said, he too had been upset.

"There is so little we can do about it," he reflected. "I had always believed, although I do not like the German race, that Helen enjoyed sitting on the throne and being the most important lady in the land."

There was no answer to that.

Latasha knew that there was nothing either of them could do for Helen, but she thought now that was not the sort of life she herself could bear.

Somehow she must avoid it at all costs.

"What can I do, Harry?" she asked. "How can you reply to your friend Prince Kraus."

The Duke made a helpless gesture with his hands.

"I don't know what to say. I can see your point of view, Latasha. Yet we both know that if the Queen insists on choosing a husband for you, it could be someone a good deal less attractive than young Stefan who, if he is anything like his brother Kraus, is certainly charming."

"And *if* he is not?"

Again her brother just put out his hands.

Latasha walked to the window.

She realised that they were both in a position when words were hopeless – there was really nothing they could say which had not been said before.

"One step at a time," suggested Harry. "Can you think of anyone as a Governess for Kraus's sister? What did he say her name is?"

He looked down again at the letter.

"Amalie. Quite a pretty name."

"You are lucky that *you* do not have to marry *her*," added Latasha somewhat spitefully.

"I agree with you, Latasha, but at least the girl will have charm like her brother or should I say brothers?"

Latasha gave a little cry.

"Now you are trying to persuade me into accepting this idiotic, stupid and quite impossible idea!"

She turned from the window and walked back to her brother.

"I want to be in love when I do marry, Harry. You know Papa always said he fell in love with Mama the first time he saw her. She said she felt something strange about him as soon as he touched her hand. Of course it was love at first sight."

"That happens only once in a million years. If you are going through your life seeking the impossible, there is every chance, my dear pretty sister, that you will end up an old maid."

"I think it would be better to be an old maid than to be married just because my husband is frightened of the Russians and I can provide him with a Union Jack!"

"He has good reason to be frightened. You cannot deny it, the Russians are behaving appallingly as everyone has said. In fact I would not like to tell you the language that is used about them in White's Club."

"I can guess what they say, Harry, but that does not make it any easier for me."

The Duke put his arm round her.

"I know that, my dearest, and I do not want to scare you. At the same time this is a very tricky problem and for the moment I cannot imagine how we can get out of it."

"We have to, Harry," muttered Latasha.

"What you really have, although we do not like to face it, is a choice between marrying a young man whose brother we know is a delightful and charming person or at any moment receiving a command from Windsor Castle."

The Duke's voice deepened as he continued,

"You will then be ordered to marry a man who we would know nothing about, who may be any age between eighteen and eighty and who wants you just as a defence to keep the Russians at bay."

"I know that, of course, I know that," Latasha cried angrily. "But why does this have to happen to *me*? There are millions of other girls in the world who are not forced up the aisle to marry a man they do not even know."

"We are privileged enough to have Royal blood in our veins. Although Mama was never that interested in her Royal relations, Royal blood is now being used to fight the Czar's policy of expansion."

He paused for a moment before he added,

"Actually the extraordinary thing is that they are afraid of us. The Czar was made to look a fool over Prince Alexander of Battenburg. The one thing he cannot afford is war with Great Britain."

"Of course you are right," asserted Latasha. "At the same time sooner or later someone will have to stand up to them."

"I agree with you, but I only hope it does not have to be me."

"For the present it seems to be *me*," sighed Latasha.

There was a note in her voice which told the Duke she was really upset.

He put his arms round her.

"Cheer up, old girl. I promise you I will do my best to try and find a way out of this mess. I admit I cannot at the moment see one – but I swear I will try."

Latasha put her head on his shoulder.

"I know you will, Harry, but I am frightened, *very* frightened."

"Try not to think about it, Latasha. Let's forget for the moment the horror of it and concentrate on finding a nice little Governess for the sixteen year old. She at least can wait another year before she is pushed into marrying someone she has never met!"

"I wonder if there is anyone in the local village who would like to go to Oldessa," said Latasha reflectively.

"Now listen, don't make a mistake about this," her brother contended. "The Prince will want someone well-bred and intelligent. After all he made a First at Oxford himself and I expect his family are as clever as he is."

"The only candidate I can possibly think of is the Vicar's daughter," retorted Latasha. "But if she leaves, who is going to play the organ on Sundays?"

Her brother chuckled.

"Now leave the village alone. Think of someone suitable you have met in London who is either poor enough or bored enough to want to visit Oldessa."

Latasha did not answer him and he so continued,

"I can assure you that it is a lovely country. Who knows, she might pick up a charming young man and it could be the greatest opportunity of her life."

"Now you are turning it into a fairy story – she will marry the dashing Prince and live happily ever after!"

"But why not? Stranger things have happened in life."

Then he saw that his sister was staring at him.

"I have an idea," she murmured. "It is stupid of me not to have thought of it before."

"What is it?" he enquired.

Latasha answered him very slowly and deliberately.

"I will go to Oldessa as the Governess for Princess Amalie. Not as myself of course, but under an assumed

17

name. It will give me the opportunity to see the situation out there and if I could like Prince Stefan enough to marry him. While I am away, Queen Victoria will not be able to marry me off."

The Duke was astonished – he could hardly believe what his sister was saying.

"You cannot mean it, Latasha," he said eventually.

"But I do mean it, Harry. Here you are, frightened, although you will not admit it, that you will have to say no to your friend Kraus or that Queen Victoria will give you an order you cannot refuse – and I have the solution."

She sank down again into her chair.

"What is it now, Latasha?"

"Let's work this out carefully – you write to Prince Kraus and say you are looking for someone who might be the right wife for Prince Stefan and you are also looking for an experienced Governess for his sister.

"But she may take a little time to find, so you are sending out temporarily a young girl you can recommend personally. She will, of course, unknown to them be *me*!"

"Do you really think you could get away with it?"

"Of course I will, Harry, I had enough Governesses myself to know how they behave and you cannot say my English is anything but perfect."

"I will grant you that."

"Thank you, my dearest brother. I won three prizes for English Literature."

"I'm only teasing."

"Well, stop being funny and help me. I must look demure, but not too dull – "

Latasha paused for a moment and then suggested,

"I think my father might be a retired Colonel who

has fallen onto hard times. I am therefore prepared to go temporarily to Oldessa because I want to see the world, but cannot afford to travel and pay for myself."

"You may find yourself in a great deal of trouble."

"What do you mean?" his sister enquired.

"I have always been told that pretty Governesses are 'fair game'. As you are extremely pretty, you may find it hard to keep the smart young men of Oldessa at bay."

"I think you may remember I am a very good shot," she countered. "Papa taught me, as he taught you, and you know how good he was."

"I have been told that by every single person on the estate and every one of his friends. I am always hoping for a few compliments for myself!"

Latasha giggled.

"You do receive quite enough compliments already from beautiful ladies telling you how wonderful you are!"

Latasha was well aware that he could have married any number of pretty young women of her age or a little older.

Their pushy mothers had been particularly anxious to capture him, not only for his title, but because he had excellent manners and outstanding possessions.

The Duke, however, had said firmly he was in no hurry.

He would marry when he had met the right person, which he had not done so far.

That suited Latasha, who liked having her brother to herself.

As soon as their mother died she had played hostess for him whenever he entertained at Norlington Park.

"I think," she now said, "I can look after myself. If I fail to do so, I shall be very disappointed."

"I don't think you can travel to Oldessa without a chaperone," the Duke objected.

Latasha laughed scornfully.

"Don't be so absurd! How can a Governess have a chaperone? I will require someone to escort me there, of course. But I expect that if you inform Prince Kraus what a suitable Governess you have found for his sister, he will send a courier who is reliable and who will bring enough money so that I can afford the Orient Express."

"I can see you intend to do it in style. At the same time if you are really ready to undertake such a strange adventure, it would certainly make my answer to Kraus a good deal easier."

"All you have to tell him is that you are trying to find someone to marry his tiresome brother. And that you are hoping to find an experienced Governess before long, and just don't mention me at all."

"I don't like it, Latasha, I am sure it is something I should not allow you to do."

"If I do get into trouble, I will just come home. If anyone assaults me or is threatening me, I will shoot them. Not to kill, but I might make them lame for a year or so!"

The Duke laughed as he could not help it.

"I think you are crazy and I think I am mad to abet you. If you desire an adventure, what you are undertaking definitely is one."

"I do think it is something I will enjoy, and what is more, if they are not standing up to the Russians, I will just tell them how cowardly they are and how important it is for them to set an example to the rest of the Balkans instead of going whining to Queen Victoria."

The Duke chuckled.

"Now I am feeling sorry for my friend Kraus. He

has no idea what is going to strike him. I am quite certain, my beautiful little sister, you will be more dangerous than any cannonball fired into the Palace!"

CHAPTER TWO

They sat talking and laughing for a little longer.

Then the Duke proposed,

"Now let's be sensible. I have been thinking while we have been making a story of all this, that quite frankly the answer is a big *no*! You are not going to Oldessa as a Governess. You either go as yourself on a visit with me or as the future bride of Prince Stefan."

The way he spoke was quite different from the way he had been talking a few minutes earlier.

Looking at her brother, Latasha realised he really meant it.

"I think you are being very tiresome, Harry, and not very helpful to your friend. But if you are absolutely intent on refusing to allow me to go as a Governess, I will think of another way."

The Duke groaned.

"I think all your ideas are crazy and I am not going to listen to them."

"Well just listen to this one, as I think it is rather clever."

The Duke sighed, but he was listening intently as she proposed,

"I think perhaps you are right that I should not go as just an ordinary Governess, because I might then be kept upstairs in a dreary schoolroom and be unable to see much of Prince Stephan or anyone else."

"That is about the first sensible thing you've said."

"So why," Latasha went on as if he had not spoken, "should I not go as someone who is important enough for the Court to be pleased to entertain, but who is not Royal enough to marry the Prince?"

"I don't understand."

"It is quite simple. You write to Kraus and say that it is most difficult at the moment to find an experienced Governess and it will take time. But a great friend of ours who lives near us is anxious to see Oldessa after all she has heard about it.

"And she would be pleased to be invited to stay for a while and give the Princess English conversation lessons while she is there."

The Duke stared at Latasha.

"Who are you suggesting should go?" he enquired.

"Do not be silly, Harry, it will be *me*, but I will not go as myself. Now let me think."

She paused for more thought.

"I will be Gloria which sounds like the sort of name that should impress the Oldessans. Lady Gloria Ford, the daughter of the Earl of Ranford, who is a great friend of yours!"

"I think you are getting madder every moment. Do you really think you can get away with a false title?"

"Of course I can. Do you really suppose they have nothing better to do than to sit and look up my antecedents in *Debrett's Peerage*? If you recommend the daughter of the Earl of Ranford, why on earth should they be anything but pleased to accept her?"

The Duke put his hand to his forehead.

"I am trying to think clearly and it is very difficult while you are making mad suggestions one after another!"

"But it is not mad," she insisted, "and I should have thought of it before. Of course you are right – if I go as a Governess I might be ignored completely, except for when I am teaching the child."

"I think that's a certainty."

"Very well, you are right, in which case I will go as someone who is almost the equivalent of myself, someone who is of good birth, but not Royal and therefore will be of no use to your Princely friend, except that I speak perfect English and will converse with his sister while I am having a good pry around to see what else happens in the Palace."

The Duke felt he had to admit that there was some commonsense in this proposal.

"You still cannot travel alone," he persisted, as if he was determined to find fault in her scheme.

"No, of course not, Harry, Lady Gloria will travel with her lady's maid and a very respectable courier. Two, if you prefer."

"And who will be your lady's maid? You do know how servants gossip. I would not mind betting that within half-an-hour of your arrival at the Palace, they would know you are an imposter and in fact my sister prying into their affairs. I am not having *that*!"

"Now you are being stupid in order to get your own way. I have no intention of taking my present lady's maid, who I do admit is a tremendous gossip. I shall take Nanny. You know we can trust Nanny with our lives. She would do anything for us just because she loves us."

The Duke lapsed into silence.

He knew that Latasha was speaking the truth.

Nanny would do anything for him or for any of the family.

She had been with them ever since Helen was born and it was impossible to think of the house without her.

"I suppose that Nanny would not mind going," he queried a little doubtfully.

"She would love it. She was saying only the other day she was sorry she had not travelled more in her life. I actually promised her that the next time I went to Paris or anywhere else on the Continent, I would take her with me. I was thinking of just a short visit while this venture might take a little longer."

She looked at her brother defiantly before adding,

"On the other hand if I find it is too horrible, I will return home at once. You can always send me a telegram to say that one of the family has died and I have to attend the funeral!"

The Duke threw up his hands.

"The whole thing is getting too complicated for me. I think the best thing would be to tell Kraus straight away that I cannot help him."

"Harry, you know you have no intention of doing anything of the sort. Prince Kraus has always been one of your best friends and you cannot let him down. Equally you know as well as I do that the right sort of Governess would be hard to find and we do not want to send a dud."

"Are you really expecting me," the Duke enquired, "to look for this Governess while you go gallivanting off to Oldessa incognito?"

Latasha clapped her hands.

"*You have got it right at last*! But you do see that this is the solution both to your problem and to mine?"

There was silence before the Duke remarked,

"I suppose it is just possible that you could pull it off, if you do not make a total mess of it."

"I am not likely to make a mess of it when there is so much at stake. I mean it is *my* predicament.

"If Prince Stefan is as charming as you make out, then I might consider marrying him. But if, as I suspect, he will be very like Helen's husband – perhaps not quite as bad as he is not a German – then I will just come home and go on praying that Her Majesty the Queen forgets my very existence."

"I think that is likely, but the Marquis of Salisbury is a clever sharp-brained man. I am certain he goes to bed at night wondering who else is available for the Balkans. It is only a question of time before he thinks of you."

"You make it sound even more unpleasant that it actually is," complained Latasha.

She spoke in a different voice from the one she had used earlier.

"Forgive me, my dearest Latasha, I am really very worried and you know, however much we joke about it, I want your happiness above everything else in the world."

"Then you do understand that I cannot be pushed off onto a man I have never seen. It might be easier for me to marry Prince Kraus, who at least I do know something about because you have spoken of him so often."

"I see your reasoning, Latasha, and in my opinion Kraus would be a perfect match for you. He is one of the nicest men I have ever known."

"But he is preparing to die and that does not help things, does it?"

The Duke walked across to the mantelpiece, then back again.

"I suppose," he conceded reluctantly, "I will have to agree to your optimistic plan to pose as a friend of the family."

"They will believe me, of course, they will believe me and I promise you that if I go as Lady Gloria Ford and find I do like Prince Stefan, I will accept him. It would be better than to come home feeling terrified every time there is a knock on the door in case it is a letter from the Marquis of Salisbury."

"If so, it will be to instruct me to come to Windsor Castle and then it will be most difficult to say I have no beautiful sister who is of marriageable age."

"You are very lucky that there are no thrones in the Balkans occupied by fat ugly women who require a nice English husband. The whole scenario is grossly unfair, but now that we have thought of a solution for the moment at any rate, sit down now and write the letter to Prince Kraus while I go and talk to Nanny."

She rose as she spoke.

Then walking to her brother she put her arms round him and kissed his cheek.

"You have to help me over all this, Harry. Heaven knows how the story will end, but at least we have each other."

The Duke held her close to him.

"You know I would do anything for you, Latasha."

She kissed him again.

She went upstairs to the old nursery where Nanny had slept and lived ever since they were small children.

Even though she was over sixty Nanny still looked comparatively young and she was always very interested in anything that her 'babies' did.

Latasha knew, although she did not say so, that she was afraid of the day when she would be married and left Norlington Park.

When she walked through the nursery door, Nanny looked up.

She was crocheting some lace to go on the ends of face towels, which she did very expertly.

"I was a-wondering when you'd be coming to see me," she muttered before Latasha could speak.

"I am so sorry, Nanny, I have rather neglected you in the last few days," replied Latasha, "but you know the reason."

"I knows it right enough, dearie, yet another horse! What it should be at your age is not a horse, but a young man."

"That is just what I have come to talk to you about, Nanny."

She sat down in the armchair beside Nanny and told her the whole story from beginning to end.

Nanny listened attentively to her and said nothing until Latasha had finished.

"What I am suggesting, Nanny dear, is that you and I go and have a look at this young man. You are a better judge of people than I am. If he is not what we want, we will just come back again with no bones broken."

Nanny did not speak at once and Latasha looked at her anxiously. Then she said,

"It's just like you to think up something fantastic. It's a very clever idea. No one can ever say it isn't and it's worth giving it a try."

Latasha gave a shout of joy.

"That is so very you, Nanny, and I knew you would understand! I think the sooner we get it all over with the better."

"I agree with you there, dearie, specially if it's true that His Grace may be sent for to go at once to Windsor Castle – "

She made a sound which was more of a sniff than a sigh and added,

"That usually ends in trouble!"

"You are quite right, Nanny. We will be leaving in a few days time and if everything in Oldessa is horrible, we will come back as quickly as we went."

Nanny looked towards the door.

"Now you be careful," she cautioned, "when you're a-talking to His Grace or anyone else. Everyone has long ears in this house and it'd be a great mistake for anyone to know you weren't going to this strange place in Europe as yourself."

"I know it. Again you are quite right, Nanny. We must not talk about it. Anyone might be listening and on no account must Harry tell his valet."

"That man has a very long tongue, dearie. He's amusing, I grant him that, but it's usually at someone else's expense."

Latasha knew there was an age-old battle between her brother's valet and Nanny.

Because Harry had been her baby, she thought she should always have the last word in everything he needed and anything new at the Park. Harry's valet quite naturally resented her interference and they were both invariably at daggers drawn.

Latasha rose to her feet.

"I am going now to see that Harry has written the letter to Prince Kraus and has made it clear that I am Lady Gloria Ford, who will soon be arriving in Oldessa with her lady's maid, who is *you*."

"It won't be anything new for me to look after you, dearie – it's what I've done for the last eighteen years."

Latasha laughed.

Nanny always had the last word and of course what she said was absolutely right.

"You are an angel to agree, Nanny," she said as she

walked to the door. "Even Harry has to admit I could not have a better chaperone."

"From what I hears in going to them foreign parts, you'll jolly well need one!"

Latasha was giggling as she walked down the stairs.

When she went into the study, she found that Harry had finished his letter and he had written exactly what she wanted.

"All I need to add," he said, "is the actual date you leave."

"Oh, as soon as possible, I hate feeling it is hanging over my head."

"Very well, Latasha, I would suggest you go next Tuesday. That gives you three days to pack, which should be enough for any woman."

"Fortunately I don't need any new clothes. When we go to London on Monday, the courier, whom of course you must engage for Lady Gloria, can then meet us at the Railway Station. It would be a mistake for him to come to Norlington House."

"Yes," agreed the Duke. "I will indeed write off at once and as I always patronise the same agency, I always get their best courier."

"You must say it is for a friend and not one of the family," Latasha warned him.

"I am not a fool," her brother retorted.

She left the room wending her way to the stables.

If she had to leave home, the thing she would miss more than anything else was the horses.

Of course there would be plenty of good horses in Oldessa, which doubtless would have come from Hungary.

But she loved those in their own stables, especially

the ones she regarded as her own and rode more often than the others.

A little later she was riding through a nearby wood.

As she did so, she wondered how she could bear to go away from England and live in another country.

She loved her home and she loved her brother and was quite certain no one else could ever take his place.

She could not imagine that any foreign Prince could understand what she felt at this moment.

She had always believed that the woods were magic and that there were fairies in them, who would eventually bring her everything she wished for.

She had always turned to the woods for consolation when she was feeling unhappy – also when she was happy, so that they could share her happiness with her.

'How can I leave you?' she implored.

She thought there was a rustle in the trees and soft movements in the undergrowth.

When she returned to the house, she remembered for the first time they had visitors for dinner that night and among them was one of their neighbours.

He was a young gentleman who had been pursuing Latasha ever since she was a schoolgirl.

He was rich with an attractive house which he had inherited from three generations of his ancestors, but it did not in any way compare with Norlington Park.

Yet Latasha, who had been there often, thought it was reasonably comfortable and pleasant, especially for a man who was not married.

His mother was alive, but spent most of her time in the South of France as the doctors thought the warmer air was better for her than the cold winter winds which would affect her lungs.

As Latasha dressed herself for dinner that night, she was thinking that it might solve every problem if instead of saying 'no' to Patrick again tonight she would say 'yes'.

He had become used to her refusing his proposals of marriage and they could even laugh about it.

The last time they had been together he had said,

"I suppose as usual I have to humiliate myself by asking my darling adorable Latasha if she will marry me."

"You know the answer," Latasha had replied.

"I hear what you say," Patrick answered her, "but I want to know why."

Latasha spread out her hands in a graceful gesture.

"I like you, Patrick, and I enjoy being with you, but to be frank, I do not love you as I want to love the man I marry."

"You have said all that before, Latasha, but suppose you never find him?"

"Then I shall just continue thinking of you as my closest and dearest friend and enjoying the times we are together."

"But that is just not enough – not enough for me. I want you, Latasha, and God knows I have been careful not to rush you or try to force you into accepting me. But we cannot go on like this."

"Why ever not?"

"Because I want to be married. I want you as my wife and I want a son to inherit my estate when I die."

"You are not going to die for a long time. I am sure as the years pass by and I grow old and ugly, you will find someone young and beautiful to spring into your arms the moment you hold them out."

"You are making a mockery of it," he complained. "I love you, Latasha, with all my heart and, as you know, since you have grown older, I have never looked at anyone else."

"But I have looked at quite a lot of men and none of them are exactly what I want."

"What do you really want?" enquired Patrick.

"You know the answer – someone who makes my heart beat quicker. I want someone I will love not only for a short time but for the rest of our lives together."

"That is exactly what you do to me."

He held out his arms.

However, Latasha, who had had this conversation with him many times before, managed to evade them.

"Please allow me to kiss you," he implored, "and I will make you feel as you want to feel about love."

"I made a vow that I would never let a man kiss me until I was absolutely certain that he was the right one. I have no wish to be disappointed."

"Why do you think that I would disappoint you?" Patrick persevered.

"Because at the moment you are not the right one for me. I do not know why, and perhaps it is a mistake to talk about it, but my instinct tells me that what I feel for you, although it is a feeling of deep affection, it is not the love I seek."

"But I will teach you about the love you are looking for. I swear to you I will do that and, once you understand love, it will grow and grow year by year until it fills our lives and there is nothing else for us but endless love."

Latasha drew in her breath.

"That is what I want and that is what I am seeking, but it is something you cannot force to happen and that is why, Patrick dear, although I am very very fond of you, I cannot at this moment become your wife."

Because he had been afraid of losing her he had not worried her unduly.

Although she and Patrick met frequently, they had not been alone for long enough to have long conversations without being interrupted.

Now, as she was dressing, for the first time Latasha was thinking seriously that perhaps she had been stupid to refuse Patrick.

She would be absolutely certain to stay in England by becoming his wife.

She would be near her home and it would be easy to ride Harry's horses as well as those Patrick provided for her.

She was very sure that he would keep his word and never love anyone except her.

'Perhaps I really am a fool,' she thought, 'to go on seeking the unobtainable – '

Perhaps she was reaching for the stars, but would never be able to touch them.

She could well imagine all too clearly the light in Patrick's eyes if she said that she would marry him and the excitement there would be in his household and among the servants at Norlington Park.

They would be married in the village Church where she had been christened. Her mother and father lay buried in the churchyard with a great number of their ancestors.

Then she would be able to settle down to being the most important lady in the neighbourhood – until of course Harry married and brought home a Duchess.

Yet as she thought of this prospect, she knew it was not enough.

She still wanted something more, something bigger, something she could not yet put into words.

She sensed it was there if only she could find it.

During the dinner party there was no chance at all of talking to Patrick privately.

But the next morning she felt that she could not go abroad without telling him something, so she sent a groom to ask if she could see him that afternoon.

Patrick was waiting for her in his garden.

As he was a keen gardener himself it was almost as large and as beautiful as the one at Norlington Park.

When he saw Latasha walking towards him through his roses, he threw down his hoe.

He hurried towards her with outstretched hands.

"I somehow knew that you would come and see me this afternoon, Latasha. I told you, I have an instinct where you are concerned."

"I have really come to say goodbye, Patrick."

"*Goodbye*!" he exclaimed. "Where are you going?"

"We are going to London on Monday morning and then I am going to cross the Channel to spend a week or so in Paris with some friends."

"There will be so many men there telling you how beautiful you are, but I will be waiting for you when you come home."

Latasha smiled.

"I know, Patrick. And I know too that if ever I was in trouble or difficulty you would always help me."

"You know as well as I do, Latasha, I am waiting for that to happen. Then I will have a chance to show you how happy we can be together. And how safe you will be from everything that could upset or frighten you."

"There are not too many of them when I am in the country with Harry."

"Harry will have to marry one day soon. He cannot go on for ever without an heir for Norlington Park and all his other possessions including his horses."

Latasha gave a little laugh.

"At present he is completely and happily married to his horses and so determined that he will not take anyone down the aisle."

"As you are determined as well," Patrick added in a low voice.

Latasha did not answer. She was merely looking at the flowers.

Then she moved on towards the herb garden.

Patrick's mother had fully restored the herb garden, because she felt ashamed when she went to see the one at Norlington Park and she realised how badly theirs had been neglected over the years.

Patrick had added many new species to his pretty garden that was surrounded by Elizabethan brick walls and there was also a small antique fountain.

It was playing as Latasha had walked in through the ancient gate.

The sunshine on the falling water seemed to dazzle her eyes.

"Have you added any more new plants lately?" she asked Patrick.

"Quite a lot and I want to tell you about them some time. I found something which they say is very good for curing hay fever. Another that gives one long life and one called feverfew which is, I have been assured, marvellous for curing headaches or migraine."

"They should be very much in demand. People are always complaining in London that they have a headache when they stay up late at glittering parties"

They walked round the garden looking at more of Patrick's herbs.

Latasha found it all very absorbing.

When she told him that she must return home, he sighed,

"I don't want to seem a bore, but if you do not find this mythical lover you are looking for in Paris, come back to me and let us try to be happy as I really know we would be together – for ever and ever."

He spoke so very sincerely and with an earnestness that made Latasha feel she was being unkind to him.

She gently touched Patrick's cheek.

"I love you in my own way, Patrick, and I swear if it changes to your way I will come and tell you so at once."

He smiled at her a little wryly.

"I suppose I will have to be content with that."

"I am afraid so for the moment, but thank you for being so kind to me, which you always are."

"I want to be a great deal more than kind, but I do know it is something I cannot talk you into. You will have to come to me of your own freewill."

"Maybe one day I will, Patrick, but for the moment I know it would not be right for either of us."

"It would be right for *me*," Patrick added quickly.

He lifted her onto the saddle of her horse and then he kissed her hand.

"I love you," he breathed. "Whatever happens in Paris and whatever anyone will say to you, remember that I love you with all my heart and that is the most important thing I can offer you."

As Latasha rode away, she felt somewhat guilty.

Equally she asked herself what else she could do?

She was very fond of Patrick – he was part of her life just as Harry was.

But she realised that the love she was seeking was bigger and greater in a way she could not explain than what she had yet felt for anyone.

There had been men in London who had proposed to her and those who she knew she had only to encourage and they would lay their hearts at her feet.

But they were *not* her dream man.

At the back of her mind she just knew that he was waiting out there somewhere for her if only she could find him.

As she rode over the level fields towards her home she thought that her visit to Oldessa would be an exciting adventure.

Of course it would.

If danger lurked there, that in a way made it even more desirable.

At the same time she was quite certain that she did not wish to leave the world she knew – not for any foreign parts however beautiful and however attractive.

'I am definitely English through and through,' she told herself. 'If I was a more sensible girl, I would settle down with Patrick and live, if not happily, then contented for ever after.'

Even as she considered the prospect, she knew that was not enough.

She wanted more – *very* much more!

Where she would find it was indeed a problem that only time could answer.

*

On Monday morning there was the usual fluster and excitement in setting off to London.

In the old days Latasha's father always drove from Norlington House in Park Lane to Norlington Park in the country and vice versa.

Now there was a train that could carry them all far quicker and with far less strain on the horses.

The Duke's private coach was hitched on to the fast train which departed from the station at eleven o'clock. As it was new, it was well upholstered and a smart addition to the train.

The stationmaster and his assistant saw Latasha and her brother off with much ceremony and as the train drew out of the station, the stationmaster stood at attention until they were completely out of sight.

"I suppose," she commented wryly, "I cannot take this comfortable coach with me to Oldessa?"

"You will be much more comfortable on the Orient Express," Harry counselled. "I have been longing to travel on it myself. Everyone who has travelled on it says it is quite fantastic."

"I will look forward to the Orient Express, Harry, if not to my arrival."

"I am sure a band will be playing, flags waving and an escort of the country's finest Cavalry to take you to the Palace," teased Harry.

"I wish you were coming with me – "

"I would enjoy it, except I would forget you were incognito and would undoubtedly give the game away the first time I spoke to you."

"That would be a big disaster and it would be very embarrassing to say to Prince Stefan that I have only come to look him over and see if he is good enough for me."

The Duke held up his hands.

"Oh, for Heaven's sake, Latasha. Remember that

Kraus and I are close friends. If you insult the Oldessans, I will doubtless have to fight a duel to save your honour!"

"You must certainly not do so and I swear to you, I am going to be very very careful."

She paused before she asked,

"You have ordered a courier, I suppose?"

"I had sent my secretary to London on Saturday to make sure I had the best and most reliable man available. I am quite certain you will not be disappointed or lack any of the comforts."

"That is just what I want. I will be frightened and worried until I arrive. Then perhaps it may be even worse than we anticipate – "

"Nonsense Latasha, I am certain that any Palace run by Kraus will be the perfection of comfort. He was always telling me how beautiful Oldessa is and what magnificent horses they own."

"The horses attract me far more than what the men are going to be like in that particular place!"

The Duke chuckled.

"Well you can hardly marry a horse, therefore make up your mind which would be preferable. Prince Stefan or Her Majesty's unknown choice of bridegroom."

Then Latasha blurted out,

"I thought very seriously that instead of going away I might after all marry Patrick."

"I have often wondered why you keep refusing him. I do like Patrick, but I admit I cannot help feeling that you would find him rather dull."

As her brother spoke, Latasha realised that this was actually the truth.

Life with Patrick would undoubtedly be extremely

comfortable because he was so rich, but one would know exactly what was going to happen from day to day, just as she always knew what he was going to say.

"You are quite right, Harry. I need adventure and excitement in my life and, although I would be safe and comfortable with Patrick, one would not expect him ever to have any innovative ideas such as you and I have."

"I think the trouble with you," remarked Harry, "is that you expect too much. I have often thought since you have been grown up that it was a mistake for you always to be with me and my friends who are far older than you."

"A mistake?"

"They have given you ideas which you should not have at your age. I was thinking when you were arguing the other day with that man who had just come back from India that you understood as much about the problems with Russia as he did."

Latasha laughed.

"Now you are flattering me, but actually I did think that, considering he had been there for a year, he ought to have known more about Indian religions."

"In other words you are too well-informed for your age. I think it is something you are going to find wherever you go, whether it is the country, London or Oldessa."

"Then I will just have to marry an old man," said Latasha. "So what about that King who was blind and deaf and over eighty – ?"

Harry was laughing as there was no answer to this.

As they had breakfast together, Latasha thought it was lonely to be setting off on a great adventure without someone she could talk to intelligently.

"I do wish you were coming with me, Harry," she pleaded again.

"You will be all right and if things do go wrong just send me a telegram asking how Aunt Ethel is. I shall know that is a signal for me to reply that she is on her deathbed and you must return at once or perhaps that she is already dead and you must return for her funeral."

Latasha giggled.

"You are wonderful, Harry, you always understand what I try to say. Most people, when I talk of something like that, have not got a clue as to what I mean."

"I will really miss you, Latasha. I suppose if you get married I will be lonely and driven to it too. Although, as you know, I have no wish to be tied up to anyone at the moment."

"Then as soon as I have departed, go and see one of those lovely ladies who are always writing to you and who I gather have complacent husbands who disappear to the country when they are not wanted."

Harry laughed.

"You know too much and say too much, Latasha. "Young girls should be seen and not heard and they should not know about these complacent husbands and *affaires-de-coeur*."

"I would be very stupid if I did not know about them, but they are what I want my husband to avoid when I do have one."

"You should indeed be clever and inventive enough to keep him at home."

Latasha hoped he was right.

But she could not help herself recalling what Helen had said and how dreadfully dull it was for her surrounded only by women.

'I would rather marry Patrick than let that happen to me,' she told herself with determination.

CHAPTER THREE

Latasha with Nanny in attendance and her brother arrived at Norlington House in London.

The Duke's secretary immediately informed them that everything was arranged for tomorrow morning.

"You have engaged a good courier, I do hope," the Duke asked him.

"The manager of the agency has assured me that he is the very best they employ and he will meet Lady Gloria Ford as you have requested at Victoria Station."

The Duke nodded and then he and Latasha walked into his study.

"I suppose, Latasha, you are still intent on acting out this ridiculous playhouse comedy," he enquired of her when they were finally alone.

"Having put my hand to the plough, I cannot turn back," she answered him gravely.

Then she gave a sudden cry.

"I have thought of something!"

"What can it be now, dear sister?"

"I ought to have a passport."

"I have thought of that already and you have one. You are on mine. As you may remember we used it the last time we went yachting down the coast of France."

Latasha gave a sigh of relief.

"I thought for a moment it had been forgotten."

"If you remember, at the time I obtained a passport for myself with your name on it, and one for Nanny in her own name."

"Will it be safe for me to carry a passport as Lady Latasha Ling?"

"I see no reason why not. No one will see it except the French officials at Calais and those who will come to your compartment on the train as you cross frontiers."

"You are so right and I suppose it is only because I have not travelled as much as you have that I suddenly felt panicky."

"But don't leave your passport lying about. Firstly if it is stolen, I will have to send you another and secondly people will think it rather strange that our friend the deputy Governess is pretending to be you!"

Latasha laughed.

"That will make everything even more complicated than it is at the moment."

"I agree, Latasha, but I really am beginning to think that I should be coming with you after all."

"Oh no, Harry, you are not so much worried about me as that you are missing all those magnificent Hungarian horses which Prince Kraus has been boasting about in his letters."

"Perhaps you are right," the Duke sighed. "But for Heaven's sake, Latasha, take care of yourself."

He expressed the same worry the next morning as they drove to the Railway Station.

The Duke had decided that there was no need for a second carriage with a servant and the luggage.

"I'll look after her, Your Grace," Nanny piped up. "She's a good girl when she wants to be. If she gets into mischief and I cannot get her out of it, I'll send you a telegram."

"I know I can trust her with you, Nanny. Now just be extremely careful of any men who are too attentive on the journey."

"You are making me expect much too much of the journey and of the Palace when I arrive," added Latasha.

The Duke would have spoken, but she went on,

"The truth is I expect to be very disappointed and come hurrying back to you, thinking that whatever comes out of Windsor Castle is preferable to what I have found in Oldessa!"

They were laughing and arguing as they had done the previous evening.

However, Latasha was well aware that her brother was really worried in case she landed herself in trouble.

There was still a feeling in England that foreigners were always up to something unattractive and the English had never really trusted any of them since the Battle of Waterloo.

When they reached the station the courier was, as they had expected, waiting for them. He was a middle-aged man who seemed intelligent and had very good manners.

The Duke had already thought out what he would say to him, so taking him on one side, he explained,

"You will appreciate that Lady Gloria is young and a friend of my sister's. She should not be travelling alone, but her father is very ill and I cannot at the moment spare the time to accompany her to Oldessa."

The courier was listening intently as the Duke went on,

"However I am sure that you will do everything in your power to see that she is comfortable and not in any way upset by other passengers on the train."

"You can leave it all to me, Your Grace. I promise you I will look after her Ladyship and see that she gets into no difficulties."

"Have you been on the Orient Express before?"

"Three times now, Your Grace, and nothing yet has happened that I could complain about."

"That is exactly what I wanted to hear," the Duke exclaimed.

He gave the man money for the journey and a large tip for himself.

As he bade his farewell to Latasha, he felt that with Nanny beside her and the courier in charge she could not come to any harm.

The ferry boat from Dover to Calais carried a large number of passengers.

The sea was calm and the sun was shining brightly, but Nanny was very insistent that Latasha should stay in her private cabin.

Latasha really would have preferred to walk about on deck, but Nanny dissuaded her.

She said it would be a mistake to be mixed up with a lot of holiday people – many had drunk a great deal to prevent themselves from being seasick.

They arrived at Calais shortly after two o'clock.

The courier found two porters to carry their luggage to the Orient Express.

Latasha looked forward to seeing the most famous train in Europe.

She had read so much about it in the newspapers and she was thus not surprised to find that it looked even more splendid than she had expected.

It was as elaborate inside as the newspapers had described. The teak and mahogany panelling with inlaid marquetry in the compartment walls and on the doors was a luxury Latasha had not seen in any other train.

The armchairs were all covered in Spanish leather embossed with gold patterning.

She had read that at night she would be supplied with '*exquisite silk sheets, the finest woollen blankets and a counterpane filled with the lightest of eiderdown*'.

When she looked round her compartment, she said to Nanny who had one next door,

"We are certainly travelling in luxury."

Nanny was already most impressed by the heavily carpeted corridors and spring-loaded roller blinds.

She was to be over-awed by the flowered curtains which were held by silk cords and tassels of gold thread.

"It's certainly good enough for a Prince, if you ask me," muttered Nanny.

Then she turned abruptly away as she felt a little embarrassed at referring to a Prince as they were on their way to scrutinise one.

As the train pulled away from the station, Latasha settled herself down comfortably in an armchair.

The adventure she had longed for had now begun!

She could not help feeling just a little apprehensive about how it would all end.

Would she return home with Nanny disillusioned and dispirited?

That would surely mean she would be obliged to do whatever the Queen might ask of her without prevarication.

Nanny became aware that she was somewhat silent and looking depressed.

"Now come along, my dearie, take your hat off and tell me now what you're going to wear for dinner. I've put a very pretty dress on top of one of the cases, but if you've set your heart on another, please tell me."

Latasha smiled.

It was just so like Nanny to bring her back to the present rather than let her speculate on the future.

She agreed to the gown that Nanny had suggested, and Nanny then hung it up in her own compartment.

They had eaten a light and not very appetising meal on the ferry.

As soon as the train had steamed some way into the countryside a smartly dressed Steward came to ask whether they would like a glass of wine or tea or coffee.

Nanny asked at once for tea whilst Latasha chose coffee.

It was served in the most attractive china and none of the etceteras like milk, cream, sugar and *petit fours* were forgotten.

Latasha had been a little afraid when they arrived at Calais there might be someone who knew her among those waiting for the train to Paris or for the Orient Express.

She had therefore hurried quickly from the ferry to the platform where their train was waiting.

Deliberately she did not look round.

She knew it would be a mistake to ignore anyone she knew, but they might easily blurt out her name in front of the courier and she could hardly tell them not to do so.

Everyone enjoyed a secret, but if they were at all human they would be seeking to find out about it and then inevitably they would pass it on to someone else.

She could hear the sound of people talking outside in the corridor, thus she stayed quietly in her compartment until it was time to change for dinner.

To her surprise, Nanny said firmly that she would not be accompanying her.

"I felt a bit seasick on the ferry, dearie, although I did not say so and to tell the truth I'm tired. If I can have something to eat here and get into bed, that's all I wants."

"Then, of course, that is what you will have, Nanny dearest."

She rang for a Steward who arrived instantly and he said it was no trouble to bring Nanny anything she chose to eat.

He produced a somewhat overwhelming menu and Latasha chose for her what she knew of old were Nanny's favourite dishes.

At eight o'clock a quiet knock on the door informed Latasha that dinner would be served in fifteen minutes.

She pulled a wrap around her shoulders and walked along the corridor.

The dining car itself definitely more than lived up to her expectations. The tables were laid with snow-white damask cloths.

The napkins were folded to look like butterflies and the cutlery was of solid silver and the plates were of gold-rimmed porcelain.

What Latasha had not expected was that the waiters wore tail-coats, breeches and silk stockings.

There was a long menu and she felt it would put on pounds of weight to anyone who ate every course.

She was shown, as soon as she arrived, to a small comfortable table for two.

As the train had not seemed to be completely full, she hoped that she could remain unnoticed and that no one would take the empty place on the other side of the table.

She was served with the first course, which she had to admit was delicious.

Then a tall man who was obviously alone came into the dining car and sat down opposite her.

He had been offered a table on the other side of the car, but had refused it, insisting on the empty chair at her table.

As he sat down Latasha realised that he was French and thought he must be about thirty years of age.

From the way in which he was dressed and the way he behaved she was certain that he considered himself of some importance.

She deliberately did not look at him but down at her plate and occasionally she turned her head to look out of the window.

She became aware that he was watching her.

They must have sat there in silence for almost five minutes before the newcomer began in excellent English,

"Forgive me, mademoiselle, if I introduce myself. I am Comte Estell de Fleur and I think if I am not mistaken, I have met your father on the Racecourse."

Latasha could not help being amused.

She guessed that when he had insisted on the seat opposite her, he had asked the Steward her name.

This was certainly a most original approach that her brother would find entertaining.

She was well aware that the French thought that all English gentlemen owned racehorses.

Thus there was every chance of his striking a bulls-eye with his introduction, if she was indeed the daughter of an English aristocrat.

"I am afraid you are mistaken," responded Latasha coldly. "My father is dead."

"Then naturally I must now say how sorry I am that I have not met your father, perhaps I did so when you were very much younger than you are now."

Because he had succeeded in twisting the situation around from what might have been an awkward situation, Latasha wanted to giggle.

'After all,' she thought, 'there is no reason why I should not talk to him. When I arrive at my destination, I will never see him again.'

Aloud she commented,

"You sound, monsieur, as if you have racehorses of your own."

"I have indeed, mademoiselle. At the moment I am planning to celebrate a win on the Racecourse in Paris two days ago. Will you join me in a glass of champagne?"

Latasha had not ordered herself anything to drink as she considered it would be wrong for her to drink alone.

In any case she always left the choice of wine to her brother and therefore she knew very little about wines.

"That is very kind of you," she answered demurely.

The Comte beckoned to the wine waiter and then ordered a bottle of the very best champagne.

After Latasha had been brought another course, he ventured,

"Tell me, beautiful lady, about yourself. I cannot understand, as I am often in England, why I have not been accorded the honour of meeting you before."

"Have you been racing your horses in England this Season?" Latasha asked him.

She was doing her best to ignore the compliment he had just paid her.

"I have entered one of my best horses at Ascot this year," the Comte answered, "which I am quite certain will win and I hope to run another at Goodwood."

Latasha thought that if she talked about horseracing he might discover who she really was.

She therefore remarked,

"I am afraid I know very little about racing. But I wish you success on both those occasions."

"That is most kind of you, mademoiselle, I consider I am so lucky in meeting you today when I had expected to find myself bored among a crowd of dull passengers!"

"Perhaps you are being rather unkind to them," she replied. "I have had no chance of meeting any of them as I am travelling with an elderly friend who is feeling a little seasick."

She thought, although she could not be sure, that at the mention of her friend the Comte looked disappointed.

However he raised his glass of champagne.

"I am asking you now to drink to my success on the Racecourse and to my wonderful good luck at meeting you here on the Orient Express."

Latasha felt obliged to raise her glass and touch his.

"Now for a moment we are united," said the Comte flamboyantly "and that may be a lucky omen for me in the future."

"I can only wish you good luck again at Ascot and Goodwood," repeated Latasha.

"They are in the future, but for the next few days we are in the present, so please tell me about yourself."

Latasha shook her head.

"I have been brought up never to talk to strangers and to be very discreet in what one says about oneself."

The Comte chuckled.

"There are exceptions to every rule and I would like to think that I am one of them."

He paused but as Latasha did not speak he went on,

"What is more you cannot be so unkind to me when

we are being carried away from all that is dull and ordinary into an enchanted world by what to my great surprise is a train drawn by a very modern locomotive."

He had either thought this out quickly or had used it on other occasions and it made Latasha laugh.

"I am serious, mademoiselle, I will be very hurt and distraught if we cannot spend the next day or two together, so that I can tell you how exquisitely beautiful you are."

"That is something I must not listen to," answered Latasha. "I can assure you that my father, if he was alive, would be very shocked at my talking to a stranger."

"How could you do anything else when there is just a small table between us? And I am hoping and wishing with all my heart that there will soon be nothing."

Because she was unable to think of anything to say, Latasha concentrated on her food.

She was, however, very aware that the Comte was gazing at her.

There was an expression in his eyes that she knew was dangerous.

Because Nanny was travelling with her, she had not anticipated that she would dine alone on the train.

If Nanny had now been sitting at the table with her, it would have been impossible for anyone to approach her.

"What are you thinking about, beautiful Lady?"

"I was actually thinking," Latasha responded, "that only a Frenchman could possibly pay a complete stranger so many compliments in so short a time!"

"What else can I do? You are without question the most beautiful woman I have ever seen and I assure you I have seen a great number. In fact I have paid many visits to London and enjoyed many parties I have been invited to, including those given by His Royal Highness the Prince of Wales."

"I feel sure they were most enjoyable, but I have spent most of my life in the country, which I really prefer to anywhere else."

"Then you are certainly wasting your all loveliness, mademoiselle, I am sure there are not enough men in the country to tell you how beautiful you are, so it is obviously left to me to awaken you to the fact that you are unique and a Goddess amongst women."

The way he spoke with just a slight French accent made what he was saying, Latasha felt, seem like a kind of game and it was not as embarrassing as if it had been said to her by an Englishman.

She turned to look out of the window.

The sun was sinking slowly on the horizon and the first evening star was appearing in the sky overhead.

"If we were alone in that field," the Comte carried on, "I would hold you in my arms and make it impossible for you to escape me. The one thing wrong with the Orient Express is that there are too many people on it!"

Latasha laughed.

"You can hardly expect, monsieur, to have it all to yourself!"

"But, of course, one can be alone in the luxurious compartments that have been so acclaimed in Paris."

Latasha did not respond and he continued,

"My friends have taken someone they admired or desired on a journey in this train just because they felt the compartments are more attractive than the best rooms in a hotel."

"That is a novel idea, monsieur, but I should have thought unnecessarily expensive."

"Money is not important where love is concerned, mademoiselle," the Comte answered.

Latasha had eaten her last course and refused some dessert, but accepted a cup of coffee the Steward brought.

He also tried to fill her glass with more champagne, but she refused.

"You cannot leave me," the Comte exclaimed, "to finish this delicious bottle all by myself. Shall we repair to your compartment or mine so that we might talk without being interrupted?"

"I am retiring to bed and my companion is waiting for me. She will be most perturbed if I do not join her in the next few minutes."

"Now this is ridiculous, mademoiselle, you know I want to talk to you where we can be alone and where I can tell you how alluring you are."

He spread out both his hands in a typically French gesture before adding,

"I am so captivated, bowled over and at your feet. How can you be so cruel as to leave me in such a state?"

"I expect you will soon recover," asserted Latasha lightly. "As I am tired I wish you goodnight, monsieur."

She rose as she spoke and walked out of the dining car before the Comte could prevent her.

She hurried down the corridor thinking with a sense of amusement it might be the first time his very eloquent approaches had been refused.

Her school had been attended by the daughters of a great number of foreign aristocrats and the girls had often talked about the flirtatious Frenchmen.

"They always talk about love," one said, "but they spend so much of their time with the *courtesans* in Paris, who Papa says are greedily expensive."

Latasha did not at first understand what this meant.

When she had asked her brother, he told her that she

was not likely to meet any *courtesans* and therefore the less she knew about them the better.

However her books told her more about them.

She found the descriptions of *courtesans*, especially the most famous ones like Madame de Pompadour, were fascinating.

She thought the Comte had behaved exactly as she would have expected from a flirtatious Frenchman.

She walked into her own compartment and locked the door.

It was then she remembered that tomorrow and for several more days she could not avoid seeing him again.

She wondered if he would continue to pursue her, but he might easily find someone more amenable on the Orient Express.

She took off her gown and then she went in to see Nanny.

When she knocked lightly on the door, there was no answer, so she tried to open it and found it was not locked.

Nanny had obviously been expecting her, but had fallen asleep.

She reflected that Nanny looked rather older when her eyes were closed.

She pulled down the blinds and then peeped down the corridor to make quite certain that the Comte was not wandering past, perhaps looking for her.

She remembered that when she left him, the bottle of champagne was only half empty and she felt sure that he would feel obliged to finish it.

She slipped between the silk sheets and pulled up the soft woollen blanket.

'If real life was always as comfortable as this,' she pondered, 'how happy everyone would be.'

Then she wished Harry was there to argue with her as to whether her statement was true.

Life would be too easy, he would say, if it was too soft, too comfortable and never unexpected.

She had often thought that if an outstanding horse won every race and there was no possibility of him being defeated, the excitement would not be the same.

Harry had once said to her when they were talking on very much the same theme,

"It's the birds I miss when I am out shooting that I think about afterwards, not the ones I have brought down."

'I suppose,' Latasha reflected before she fell asleep, 'that if we are to live fully, there has to be the unexpected and disappointments in one's life. Otherwise people would stop struggling to get to the top and they would merely put their feet up and take it easy.'

Once again she wished that Harry was with her and then she wondered if it would be possible to talk of such subjects seriously with someone like the Comte.

She felt certain it would be impossible as he would only be thinking about her as a pretty woman and he would not be in the least interested in her brain, nor in what she felt about life and living.

'If I married someone like him,' she told herself, 'I should be bored stiff with him in the first few days after the wedding!'

Then she remembered she was going to see Prince Stefan and she had to make up her mind whether she would marry him or, as Harry had put it so delicately, take 'pot luck' with a stranger of Queen Victoria's choice.

'How can I possibly be so involved in such a mess – such a ghastly situation?' she muttered to herself.

Suddenly she felt frightened – frightened in a way she had never been before.

Up to this moment it had seemed not to be really happening, no more than a joke that she should be going out to Oldessa.

Going to inspect a bridegroom was rather as Harry might inspect a horse he was considering buying.

Latasha suddenly had the disagreeable idea that the Orient Express as it moved speedily and smoothly on was carrying her into a trap.

One from which she would be unable to escape.

She wanted as she had never wanted so much to go home.

To run into the drawing room and find her father and mother waiting for her.

All through her life they had been her protectors and her guardians – the two most important people in her little world.

Now suddenly she was alone.

Alone on a mad journey that she was quite certain would end in disaster.

Perhaps Prince Stefan would fall into love with her and he might beseech her to marry him, while she thought him repulsive and longed to run away.

Then Harry would be annoyed because she would be offending his friend Prince Kraus.

This was another aspect of her situation she had not thought through and it might be a very important one.

If Harry, Prince Stefan and his brother Prince Kraus were all begging her to save Oldessa, what could she do?

'I have been a fool,' she told herself, 'to even think of coming here. Once they have got hold of me, they will never let me go.'

It flashed through her mind that she might get off at Strasbourg and go home.

Then, as the train rolled on, she knew she could not be a coward.

She had been brave enough in the first place to go on this venture and it was she herself who had worked out the components of the drama she was to play the lead in.

Now it was impossible to back out.

If it all ended in disaster, there would be no one to blame except herself.

Quite suddenly she felt small and defenceless in a large and overwhelming world.

She wanted someone to protect her and to look after her and if at all possible someone to love her.

'I suppose it is just what all women really desire,' she thought scornfully.

Nevertheless it was true.

Perhaps it was the Orient Express, perhaps it was the Comte, but she was feeling deeply apprehensive.

The only thing left was to pray that God would help her and she found herself saying the prayers she had said when she was small.

Somehow she knew that there was only one person on whom she could depend and that was God Himself.

*

In the morning Latasha woke up feeling much less despondent.

She felt rather ashamed of herself for giving way to fear.

When Nanny came into her compartment looking neat, tidy and capable, Latasha greeted her,

"I am so glad to see you, Nanny. You were asleep when I came to say goodnight."

"I'm sorry, dearie. I was that tired and just dropped off. When I woke it were morning."

Latasha laughed.

"You are very lucky. Most people would lie awake like I did, worrying and wishing we had not come on this wild escapade."

"Now don't you talk such silly nonsense. It's better than staying back at home and crying over spilt milk. Who knows, things might be much better than we now expect."

"That is so like you, Nanny. I feel I am back in the nursery. I have made a mess of my dress and you are now singing me a lullaby which always sent me to sleep!"

"Well instead of singing you a lullaby I suggest you get up and we go along to breakfast."

"I had forgotten about breakfast. Shall we have it in here or in the dining car?"

"Well you might be content with a cup of tea, but I'm that hungry," replied Nanny. "And I'd so like to see this dining car as I've heard so much about it."

Immediately Latasha jumped out of bed and Nanny helped her to dress.

She wondered if she should tell Nanny about what had happened last night and then she thought it would be a mistake.

The mere fact that Nanny was with her would make it impossible for the Comte to sit down at the same table.

It would be best if she just kept out of his way.

She was certain that if he had been able to escort her to her compartment and found it empty, he would have tried to kiss her.

Latasha had no intention of allowing him or anyone else to do so.

Once again it flashed through her mind that perhaps she would never be kissed by anyone she really loved.

Almost as if Nanny could understand her thoughts she prompted,

"Now come along, dearie, and stop worrying. It's no use you fussing before we arrive about what's going to happen. We should be saying a prayer that this train don't run off the line or into another one!"

"It is far too prestigious for that, Nanny. Think of the money they have spent on it and the fuss that has been made over it. The newspapers have talked more about the Orient Express than about any ship we may have launched in the last few years."

"That's true, but if you asks me, people should be staying at home and a-looking after their families, if they have them, rather than gallivanting round the world making trouble in those countries they goes to."

"You must not say that when everyone is trying to make the world smaller, so that we know more about our neighbours than we have ever known before."

"Well I just wants my neighbours to be my kith and kin and that's the truth. I find them foreigners a bit soft in the head. If you asks me, that's just what they are!"

Latasha was chuckling again, as they walked down the corridor to the dining car.

The table she had sat at last night was unoccupied and the same Steward showed her and Nanny into it with a flourish.

There was no sign of the Comte and she suspected he was breakfasting in bed – it was something she might have done if she had been with anyone except for Nanny or Harry.

Breakfast in England was almost as important as dinner.

Latasha had often heard her mother say,

"Ladies and gentlemen always come down for the first meal of the day properly washed and dressed and do *not* sip coffee and eat a few crumbs in their bedrooms."

She was more than aware that the French thought breakfast of no importance as a meal, while the Germans would eat enormous amounts of meat as soon as they were awake and on their feet.

She and Nanny ordered scrambled eggs and bacon followed by toast spread with marmalade.

Nanny drank tea while Latasha enjoyed a steaming cup of coffee.

"We are being so English and I suppose you know, Nanny, that when we are abroad we should do exactly as the foreigners do and not enjoy a large meal at breakfast."

"Foreigners don't know how to behave! If you asks me why Englishmen are tall and strong, it's because they eat a good breakfast as their mothers told them to do and then have meat for luncheon."

"I expect you are quite right, Nanny, but it will be so interesting to see what our new friends in Oldessa do. From what I have gathered from Harry, they are a law unto themselves and have no intention of being dictated to by the French or the Austrians, and least of all, the Russians."

"And very right too," exclaimed Nanny. "I'd never trust them Ruskies. From what I hears of their behaviour it's time Her Majesty, Queen Victoria, gave them a piece of her mind!"

Latasha remembered Nanny had been as indignant as everyone else when the story of the Russians treatment of Prince Alexander was published in every newspaper.

She was quite sure it had been as much discussed in the servant's hall as in the dining room.

Everyone had agreed that the Russians were simply

barbarians and the sooner someone like the British taught them a lesson the better.

Then Latasha wanted to shy away like a horse from her thoughts. It seemed to her that whatever she was doing, it always came back to the same question.

Should she stand up to the Russians as Harry was asking her to do?

If she refused to do so, would she be able to refuse Queen Victoria?

"I hate the Russians," she called out, speaking her thoughts aloud.

"Don't you worry about them Ruskies, my dearie," soothed Nanny from the other side of the table. "They're a bad lot and they'll get their desserts sooner or later! You mark my words."

CHAPTER FOUR

When they had finished breakfast, the courier came to Latasha's compartment to apologise most profusely for the previous evening.

"I had no idea that Mrs. Holten was not dining with you, my Lady," he said, "otherwise I would have been with you."

"She was rather tired as she had felt seasick on the ferry," explained Latasha.

"It was very remiss of me not to make certain that you were together," the courier apologised, "but you will not be worried again by the Comte."

Latasha looked at him in surprise.

"How do you know about him?"

"One of the Stewards told me that he had insisted on sitting at your table in the dining car and he has a most unsavoury reputation – "

"I had rather guessed that!"

Latasha wondered as she spoke if she would have had trouble with the Comte even if Nanny had been with her.

Then the courier added,

"I have made quite certain, my Lady, that he will not trouble you again."

"How can you be sure?" Latasha asked curiously.

"I spoke to him."

"And what did he say?"

"I said that your Guardian was of great importance in the Jockey Club and if you were upset, it might make it difficult for him to run his horses in English races."

Latasha laughed.

She thought it very clever of the courier to be so knowledgeable about the Comte.

And to know how to put him firmly in his place.

She did not say anything about it, but last night, just when she was beginning to feel a bit sleepy, she had heard a knock on the door of her compartment.

She did not answer it or make any sound and a few moments later the knock came again.

When once again she made no response, she heard footsteps receding down the corridor.

She was quite certain that it was the Comte.

She told herself he was of no consequence, but she had felt a little nervous in case he made a scene.

Now the courier had brilliantly disposed of him!

*

The next two days passed very comfortably and the food was delicious.

Nanny managed to take every meal in the dining car with Latasha.

The train stopped for a short time at Strasbourg and again at Munich and shortly after that Latasha realised they had crossed the Austrian border.

Finally the train drew into Budapest.

The courier had already told them that was where they had to leave the Orient Express.

By this time Latasha felt she had a real affection for this very special train and her journey was something she would never forget.

She had already asked her brother what she should tip the Stewards who looked after her and Nanny.

They had been extremely kind and attentive and so she doubled what he had told her to give them.

As they climbed down the steps onto the platform, Latasha felt an urge to turn round and go home.

She had no wish to face what lay ahead.

The courier took them across the station to where another train was waiting to carry them to the South and it seemed very primitive after the luxury, comfort and beauty of the Orient Express.

Latasha and Nanny were shown into a carriage by the stationmaster.

When they set off, Latasha had her first glimpse of Hungary and she was absorbed by the intense beauty of the country.

There were endless high mountains with snow on their peaks and huge rivers as well as small streams.

More than once she had a glimpse of what she was certain were the famous Steppes, where she had longed to gallop on a spirited Hungarian stallion.

It was growing late in the afternoon when finally they reached what the courier had informed them was the nearest Railway Station to Oldessa.

He also said that there would be someone to meet them.

Nanny tidied Latasha's hair and arranged her pretty decorated hat.

She had already put on one of her smarter dresses with a neat coat to wear over it, but as it was so warm she took it off at the last minute.

She stepped down onto the platform with a rustle of silk lace-edged petticoats under her summer gown.

There was an *aide-de-camp* to meet them with an open carriage drawn by two well-bred horses.

The courier followed in another carriage with the luggage and Nanny.

"His Royal Highness asked me to welcome you, my Lady," the *aide-de-camp* greeted her, "and to give you his apologies for not coming to meet you in person. But, as I expect you know, he has not been very well."

"The Duke told me and I am very sorry to hear it," responded Latasha.

"His Royal Highness is looking forward to meeting you and making your acquaintance, my Lady, and so, of course, is Princess Amalie."

"And I am looking forward to seeing your beautiful country and I can see at a brief glance it is certainly very lovely."

Latasha was not exaggerating.

Everywhere there were flowers, blossom and trees with fields full of wild flowers growing in the grass.

The houses they passed were most attractive and there were several small rivers on which there were boats and barges.

Latasha looked at the people and she was thinking she would learn by the way they were dressed whether they were prosperous or poverty-stricken.

As they drove by, the children seemed plump and well-fed and the men and women moving about the streets seemed smiling and happy.

"I am longing to learn about your country," she told the *aide-de-camp*. "It seems not only to be beautiful but prosperous as well."

"We are fortunate, my Lady, to have rich deposits of minerals in all the mountains and His Royal Highness has been very astute in extracting them more quickly than has ever been achieved in the past."

"How did he manage it?" enquired Latasha.

"With modern efficient new machinery," came the reply. "And because His Royal Highness invites experts from all over Europe to visit and advise us."

"It's a pity that everyone does not do the same. I believe some of the Balkan countries are very poor."

"That is because they are badly ruled," the *aide-de-camp* said, "and we are very lucky in having Prince Kraus as our Ruler. We are only perturbed as he is not as strong and healthy as he should be."

Latasha was longing to ask questions about Prince Stefan, but she felt it best to keep silent for the moment.

However, after they had travelled several miles she saw three men in the distance.

They were riding very fast across what seemed to be more Steppes.

The *aide-de-camp* followed her line of sight.

"That, my Lady, is Prince Stefan accompanied by two of his friends. They are trying out horses they will ride in what you in England would call a steeplechase."

Latasha smiled and commented,

"You speak very good English."

"I was fortunate enough to go to a Public School in England. It has become very fashionable in Oldessa for the aristocracy to send their sons to England after His Royal Highness attended Oxford University."

"I wonder, as you speak so well, why you have not been teaching Princess Amalie. I expect you know that His Royal Highness has asked the Duke of Norlington to find an English Governess for her. But it is rather difficult at the moment, I gather, to find the right sort of Governess."

"I can appreciate that," replied the *aide-de-camp*.

"So I am prepared," Latasha informed him, "to give her some lessons in conversation while I am staying with you."

"We think it is an excellent idea, my Lady, and you will find Her Royal Highness to be a very eager pupil. She has been putting off learning languages, because the only available teachers are dull and all getting on for sixty or more."

Latasha laughed.

"That does not sound very encouraging at all for the Princess."

They were now entering a large City and Latasha guessed this was where the Royal Palace would be.

The roads were all bordered with trees and the pink and white blossom falling from them made pretty patterns on the ground.

She had a quick glimpse of quite expensive looking shops and restaurants with many tables outside covered by sunshades.

After they had crossed a silver river, Latasha caught her first sight of the Royal Palace.

It was high above the City surrounded by trees and even in the distance she could see a profusion of flowers.

Built of white stone it looked delightfully romantic and almost as if it had stepped out of a fairytale book.

"What a lovely Palace!" she exclaimed.

"I thought that your Ladyship would admire it," the *aide-de-camp* smiled. "We Oldessans are so very proud of our Royal Palace and our Ruler and we hope never to lose either of them."

Latasha knew exactly what he was intimating.

She felt for a moment as if there was a dark shadow falling in front of her eyes.

Then she asked herself why anyone should want to disturb such a beautiful and successful country.

It was filled with what she could easily sense must be happy and peaceful citizens.

Even as she asked herself these questions, she had a glimpse in the far distance of the high mountains.

Then she knew the answer – it was *greed*.

Greed that was making the Russians scheme to take over so many of the Balkan countries.

They drove up a drive with flowers on either side and there were two enormous fountains playing in front of marble steps leading up to the front door.

As the carriage rumbled to a stop, liveried footmen ran a red carpet down the steps.

As Latasha descended from the carriage and began to walk slowly up the steps, she could see that there were several men waiting for her when she reached the top.

It turned out that they were the Lord Chamberlain and two more *aides-de-camp*.

There was no sign of Prince Kraus.

They all bowed to Latasha and welcomed her in the flowery language of Oldessa.

Suddenly a young girl ran breathlessly through the doorway.

"Forgive me, do forgive me," she cried, speaking in her own language, "I did not realise it was so late and it is rude of me not to have been on top of the steps to greet you."

She held out her hand to Latasha who curtsied.

"It is so kind of you to come, and I have been so looking forward to meeting you."

"I am delighted to be here," said Latasha.

She had learnt on the train from the courier that the language she had learned to speak in Budapest was very much the same as that spoken in Oldessa.

She had visited Budapest a long time ago with her father and mother and had never forgotten how interesting it had been.

Nor had she forgotten the language she had listened to when they took her to the theatre.

However she thought it would be a mistake if she did not speak to Princess Amalie in English and as she did so, she became aware that the young girl could understand most of what she was saying.

They walked into the Palace and it was as beautiful as Latasha thought it would be.

It had been furnished with exquisite taste and she recognised that a great deal of it had come from France.

There were statues that could only have come from Greece, but what entranced her more than anything else was that there were flowers everywhere.

She reflected how thrilled her mother would have been if she had seen them.

They had arrived late in the afternoon and were not expected to ask for English tea at such an hour.

Instead Latasha and Nanny were both given a glass of delicious local wine and there were *pâté* sandwiches and other small delicacies to eat in what was obviously one of the main reception rooms.

Princess Amalie chatted away asking them about their journey.

"I am longing to go on the Orient Express too," she enthused. "My brother Kraus has promised to take me."

She put her head on one side as she added,

"Perhaps after you have stayed with us you will ask me to come and stay with you in England. That is exactly what I would really love to do."

Latasha smiled.

"Your English will have to be very good, because English people are not intelligent like you and usually can speak only one language. If people do not understand what they are saying, they usually just shout louder!"

The *aide-de-camp* laughed out loud at this remark, but it took Princess Amalie a few minutes to see the joke.

As time was getting on the Lord Chamberlain came to ask if they would like to see their bedrooms.

He escorted them up the stairs and then he handed them over to an impressive-looking elderly housekeeper.

Latasha's room was delightfully lovely.

But she realised it was not as large and as grand as the one she would have been given if they had known her true identity.

Nanny was next door.

Their luggage had already been taken upstairs and was being unpacked by the housemaids.

"We will try to give your Ladyship everything you require," said the housekeeper, "and you have only to ask me or one of the maids."

Latasha thanked her and then she went next door to find Nanny.

"I'm being treated just like a Queen," cooed Nanny, "that I am."

"I think it is very kind of them to put you next to me, Nanny. Otherwise I am sure you would have found it very difficult to make them understand what you want."

"I'm no use and that's a fact when it comes to them

German sounding languages. But I expects I'll get what I wants."

"I am sure you will," smiled Latasha.

When she went back to her own room she found the maids were bringing in a bath for her.

They placed it on the rug in front of the fireplace, while the housekeeper was watching them do it and giving instructions.

"I am afraid my companion, who has looked after me for many years, is not able to speak your language."

"Don't worry about that," replied the housekeeper. "His Royal Highness's valet speaks English, Russian and several other languages as well."

"That must be amazingly useful."

"He tries to teach us, but I'm too old to change my ways. As His Royal Highness says, it's so important for Princess Amalie to learn English."

"I am sure she will soon learn, because she seems a very intelligent girl."

"She's that for sure," agreed the housekeeper. "But that's not to say she doesn't like having her own way."

"I think we are all a bit like that," smiled Latasha.

She had finished her bath and was wondering when she would meet Prince Kraus when an *aide-de-camp* came to escort her down the stairs to a reception room.

Latasha longed to ask him if there were any other guests, but she felt it might seem too inquisitive.

He asked her about her journey from England as they walked down the stairs.

When he opened the door into the reception room, she had no idea whom she was about to meet.

The Lord Chamberlain came over to greet her.

"I hope, Lady Gloria," he began, "you are feeling rested after your long journey and you have been provided with everything you require."

He spoke in good but rather pedantic English and Latasha thanked him.

He then led her towards the mantelpiece.

In front of it was standing a tall, very good-looking young man.

Latasha was sure as soon as she looked at him that he must be Prince Stefan.

She was right.

As the Lord Chamberlain introduced her to him she curtsied and he greeted her,

"Welcome to Oldessa. We are always delighted to have English visitors, especially those who were so kind to my brother when he was living in England."

"I have heard so much about His Royal Highness from the Duke of Norlington," replied Latasha. "I believe they were very good friends."

"They were indeed," said Prince Stefan. "But I, for some reason I have never really understood, was sent to Cambridge University instead of Oxford."

"So Your Royal Highness knows England well."

"Not as well as I would like to, but I must be honest and say I find Paris more enjoyable."

There was a glint in his eye as he spoke.

It told Latasha that what he had learnt in Paris was not just the language as part of his education.

This thought was confirmed when a few moments later the door opened.

A most attractive and elegant woman, exceedingly smartly dressed, now entered.

She was introduced as Madame le Telbé and there was no doubt that Prince Stefan found her very alluring.

He talked to her all through dinner, whilst Latasha, who was on his other side, was forced to converse almost entirely with the Lord Chamberlain.

She found him an interesting and intelligent man and she guessed without his saying anything to her that he was irritated by Prince Stefan's behaviour.

At the same time she could recognise why he found Madame le Telbé so attractive.

Like all the sophisticated French women, she flirted with every man to whom she was talking with her eyes, her hands and her lips.

By the end of the excellent meal Latasha could well understand the Prince's infatuation.

She learnt from the Lord Chamberlain that Madame le Telbé was the wife of a French diplomat who had been recalled to Paris for an important meeting.

Rather than stay alone in the Embassy Madame had moved into the Palace.

Princess Amalie had also come down to dinner and she was chatting away happily to two of the younger *aides-de-camp*.

Dinner had not yet finished when she came running to Latasha's side to say goodnight.

"I have to go to bed now," she sighed. "It's a lot of nonsense and I should be allowed to stay up a bit later, but Kraus insists that I should retire before dessert is served."

"What are you planning to do tomorrow morning?" Latasha asked her.

"What do you want to do?" the Princess enquired.

"I don't know if I dare suggest what I would really like," replied Latasha with a smile.

"I always go riding before breakfast," the Princess informed her.

"Could you arrange for me to come with you?"

"Yes, of course I will, and I will show you all the best places to ride and also, if you are a good rider, there are some exciting jumps."

"I would love it. What time do we go?"

"Will eight o'clock be too early?"

"I will be ready if you will come and fetch me from my room. Remember I don't yet know my way round the Palace."

"Of course, I will fetch you," said Princess Amalie.

"It can be your very first lesson. We will talk about horses and riding in English."

The Princess giggled.

"You will talk and I will listen!"

Then before Latasha could say anything more, she ran away to kiss her brother Stefan goodnight.

"The Princess is a very attractive girl," Latasha said to the Lord Chamberlain.

"I am so glad you think as we do," he answered her. "She is adorable, but she has had a very dull time with her elderly Governesses."

"Surely there must be girls of her own age whom she could be with?"

"It is not very easy," replied the Lord Chamberlain. "The few we would like to ask are not of the right age and the others are not exactly what we might call 'in the Royal circle'."

Latasha grinned.

"I do know what you mean."

Then as she could restrain her curiosity no longer, she asked the Lord Chamberlain,

"When am I to be granted the pleasure of meeting His Royal Highness, Prince Kraus?"

"I thought you might think it strange that he did not come down to dinner. Ever since he was wounded by those Russians, he has suffered frequent headaches and migraine. The doctors seem helpless to do anything about it."

The Lord Chamberlain glanced at the clock on the mantelpiece.

"I rather think, however, you could meet His Royal Highness for a few minutes before he retires to bed. He is dining in his own rooms because he thought, as he can eat only very little, he would only spoil the party in the dining room."

"I would be so delighted to meet him and I have a great number of messages for him from his old friend the Duke of Norlington."

"Which I do know His Royal Highness is waiting to hear," the Lord Chamberlain exclaimed.

He beckoned to an *aide-de-camp* and spoke to him quietly and the man left the room.

Dessert and coffee had been served to everyone and the gentlemen were now drinking liqueurs.

Latasha had already learned from her brother that in Oldessa the ladies did not leave the gentlemen after dinner as they did in England.

For another twenty minutes they all remained in the dining room and then someone made a move.

Latasha thought it was Madame le Telbé, and they rose and walked towards the door.

As Latasha did so the Lord Chamberlain whispered,

"If your Ladyship will please come with me, I will take you to meet His Royal Highness Prince Kraus, who I understand is feeling a little better."

By this time Latasha was feeling rather curious as what was happening was not what she had expected.

Prince Stefan had paid very little attention to her all evening and she felt that he was not interested that she was English – even though in a very short period of time he might be presented with an English wife.

The Lord Chamberlain led Latasha along a broad passage and it was some distance from the drawing room.

They arrived at a large oak door with two sentries on guard outside and an *aide-de-camp* appeared and came hurrying up to the Lord Chamberlain.

"His Royal Highness is expecting you," he said.

The Lord Chamberlain nodded,

"Announce her Ladyship, but I think it is a mistake for there to be too many people in the room at one time."

The *aide-de-camp* nodded and then opened the door in front of them, proclaiming,

"Lady Gloria Ford, Your Royal Highness."

Latasha walked past him and heard the door close behind her.

She was now in an extremely attractive study which would have delighted her father.

There were pictures of horses on the walls and also a great number of cases containing leather-bound books.

The armchairs and sofas were covered in a pretty deep pink velvet whilst the curtains and the flowers were pink as well.

They made the whole room seem to glow like a setting sun.

Seated in an armchair before an exquisitely carved mantelpiece was a gentleman.

When Latasha reached him, he rose to his feet with some difficulty.

He was tall and broad-shouldered and she thought as she looked at him that he was one of the most handsome men she had ever seen.

At the same time he looked decidedly ill.

There were deep lines under his eyes and his face was pale and somewhat strained.

"You must please forgive me, Lady Gloria," he said as Latasha curtsied, "for not personally meeting you when you arrived. I have been confined to my room."

"I am sure that Your Royal Highness should not be standing now. Please sit down."

Prince Kraus smiled as if amused.

But he did as she had told him and she sat in a chair next to him.

"Did you have a good journey here, Lady Gloria?" he enquired.

"It was delightful and I was naturally enchanted by the Orient Express."

"Everyone here has been talking so much about the Orient Express. I am finding it extremely annoying that I am not well enough to travel on it myself."

"It is luxury at its height and one feels it should be kept entirely for Royalty!"

Prince Kraus laughed.

"Few people would agree with you. Now tell me about England and how is my friend, Harry Norlington?"

"He is well and his horses, as you can imagine, are still superb and the very best."

"I hope you will say the same about mine."

"I have already arranged to ride tomorrow morning, Your Royal Highness, with Princess Amalie. I have told her that it will be the occasion for her first English lesson."

"You are certainly wasting no time, Lady Gloria."

He was looking at Latasha in an unusual way which made her hope he was admiring her.

She also hoped that she was not taking too much on herself too soon.

As if he could read her thoughts, he ventured,

"I know you can only spare me a short time here in Oldessa, so please make all the arrangements you wish and just tell the Lord Chamberlain and everyone else to carry them out."

"That is a big order, Your Royal Highness, I only hope that when I have finished with Princess Amelie that you will approve of my instruction."

"I am quite certain I will, Lady Gloria, now tell me more about Harry."

Latasha told him about all the improvements her brother had made on the family estate and about the horses he had bought recently and those he was teaching to jump.

She was aware as she was speaking to him that he was listening to every word.

All the time his eyes were on her.

When she came to the end of her account, she said,

"Now I have a great many questions I would like to ask Your Royal Highness about your own lovely country. I have never seen anything so beautiful as when we drove from the station to the Palace and the flowers thrilled me."

"As indeed they thrilled my mother and it was she who insisted that the Royal Palace should be surrounded by flowers, and that if we planted them, the people in the town must plant flowers too."

"Do they appreciate them?" enquired Latasha.

"I think so. We are known here as the 'Kingdom of

Flowers' amongst our friends and I can only hope and pray it will be left as it is."

Latasha knew that he was thinking of the Russians.

Although she thought it was too soon, she could not help herself enquiring,

"What is the present situation? Harry told me that you were frightened."

"*Very* frightened, to be honest," he replied. "The only possible way we can survive will be for Harry to find what I have him asked for. That is a wife for my brother who is related to Her Majesty Queen Victoria."

He was being very frank and Latasha added,

"Harry fully understands the problem and is doing his best and he asked me to tell you so."

"Then I am absolutely certain that Harry's best is exactly what I really need."

As Prince Kraus was speaking his eyes suddenly closed and his head fell back against the cushion behind him.

"You are in pain!" cried Latasha without thinking.

"It's this ghastly migraine," he murmured.

Now there was a deep frown on his forehead and he squeezed his eyes as if the pain was almost unbearable.

Latasha rose to her feet.

Going behind Prince Kraus's chair, she placed her hands very gently on his forehead.

"Try to relax," she urged. "I am going to massage your forehead gently and I hope it will take away the pain."

She spoke very quietly.

At the same time she started to move her fingers as her mother had shown her over his forehead and down by his temples.

She had seen her mother doing it so often to people who had come to her from the village.

In fact they would come from all over the County to ask for herbs from her herb garden and to tell her of their aches and pains.

Sometimes there was such a large crowd to see her mother that her father would expostulate,

"*Really*, my darling, you wear yourself out on these tiresome people. Why do they not go to their doctor?"

"No doctor can give them what I can give them," the Duchess responded to him quietly. "Doctors' medicine is artificial, whilst mine is completely natural coming from nature itself."

Prince Kraus did not say anything and as Latasha continued to massage his head very very gently, she felt him begin to relax.

He was no longer tense with pain.

She remembered exactly the movements her mother had made on a sufferer's head.

As she used her fingers she prayed as her mother had always done.

"What I have to do, darling," she said when Latasha was still very young, "is first to pray that the person I am treating will get well. That is half the battle against illness. Secondly my own inward vitality flows from my fingers to help those who need it."

It had been made very simple for her when she was little and she had always remembered what her mother had taught her.

She felt Prince Kraus sink lower in his chair and in no way did he try to resist the life force she was passing into his body.

She had been massaging his forehead for a quarter-of-an-hour when she realised that he had fallen asleep.

She took her hands away and stood looking down at him.

He was sleeping peacefully and she was certain that she had taken the migraine away from him.

She tiptoed silently to the door and the moment she reached it, it opened.

She walked outside to find the same *aide-de-camp* who had introduced her to Prince Kraus.

"His Royal Highness is now asleep," she told him, "and is no longer in pain. Do not wake him, and if he stays there all night it does not matter. It would be a mistake to take him upstairs and make him move too quickly."

The *aide-de-camp* nodded.

"I understand, my Lady, and we are very grateful to you for helping His Royal Highness."

"Now I would very much like to meet your Head Gardener tomorrow morning immediately after I have been riding with Princess Amalie."

"The Head Gardener!" he cried in astonishment.

"*Yes*, your Head Gardener," Latasha repeated.

She knew that he was full of curiosity, but she said nothing more as they walked back to the drawing room.

As they neared the drawing room she could hear the sound of voices and laughter, but Latasha had no wish to join them.

She wanted to think of how she could help Prince Kraus, knowing how much it would please her brother.

Besides that she felt extremely sorry for him.

It was cruel, she thought, that such a handsome man should be crippled because he had fought so bravely for his country.

'I am quite sure if I can remember everything that

Mama would have done, I can make him well,' she told herself as she reached her bedroom.

She had already said goodnight to the *aide-de-camp* downstairs.

She entered her room to find, as she had expected, her nightgown was laid ready for her.

Nanny had gone to bed early on her instructions

"You are not to sit up for me," she told her firmly. "Just leave everything ready and if I am in any trouble, I will call you. Otherwise it will worry me if I think you are sitting here sleepy and I am enjoying myself downstairs."

Nanny had laughed, but she did not argue.

Latasha walked to the window and pulled back the curtains a little.

Outside there was moonlight and the sky was filled with stars.

She could see a large garden melting away into a mass of trees.

It looked lovely in the moonlight and she thought it would be even lovelier tomorrow.

'The Kingdom of Flowers,' she reflected to herself, 'yet its Ruler is not well enough to enjoy his realm.'

She looked up at the sky.

'Help him, Mama,' she prayed. 'Let me make him well so he can defy the Russians and keep this little Garden of Eden as lovely as it is now.'

It was a prayer from deep in her heart and she felt as if it winged up to the stars.

Somewhere amongst them her mother was telling her that was what she would be able to achieve.

This was clearly the *real* reason that she had been brought to Oldessa.

Latasha slept peacefully that night.

*

She was somewhat surprised when Nanny woke her at half-past seven.

"I've been told you're going riding," she said, "and if you don't hurry you'll be late."

It was the way Nanny always spoke and Latasha laughed sleepily as she climbed out of bed.

"I have so much to tell you, Nanny, but it will have to wait until I come back."

"Well, I don't suppose it'll run away, dearie, and as it's a lovely day you'd better wear your smartest habit."

"I hope you had a good dinner last night," Latasha asked Nanny as she finished washing.

"It were interesting, they're nice people but they're all scared half to death of them Russians and who'll blame them!"

'They will be safe enough if I was to marry Prince Stefan,' mused Latasha. 'But he is not interested in me.'

"I've heard all about this from the kitchen," Nanny continued. "As I've told you many times before, you never can trust them foreigners, especially the French!"

It made Latasha think of the French Comte when he had insisted on dining with her on the Orient Express and if the courier had not made certain that he left her alone, he would have continued to pursue her.

She wondered if Madame le Telbé's husband knew she was flirting so openly with Prince Stefan.

Perhaps he had some charmer of his own in Paris.

'I know one thing,' she told herself, 'I have no wish to marry a Frenchman. One would never expect him to be faithful, while at least the English do try!'

Once again she was thinking of Prince Stefan and she wondered if it would be possible for her ever to love him.

It was a question which inevitably was in her mind from the moment they met.

He was certainly very good-looking, but he seemed to her somehow extremely young – not only from the way he looked but the way he behaved.

An older man, she thought, would have been more correct in his behaviour to her at dinner.

Prince Stephan was like a young boy, determined to gather all 'the fruits off the tree'. He did not have a thought for anything but his own pleasures and amusement.

'He is very immature and, of course, he will learn,' she reflected.

Yet somehow she could not imagine him ruling the country or keeping it as beautiful and serene as it was now.

It was exactly eight o'clock when Princess Amalie came to collect her as they had arranged.

She gave a cry of joy as she came into the room.

"You are coming! You are *really* coming! I was so worried you might change your mind."

"Of course I am coming riding," answered Latasha. "Are we going alone?"

"No, Stefan is outside with the horses and we must not keep him waiting."

"Of course not."

They ran down the steps together and Latasha saw to her surprise and delight that there were two magnificent stallions held by grooms and waiting for them outside.

Prince Stefan was mounted and obviously anxious to move off.

He lifted his hat when he saw Latasha and she gave

him a wave of her hand before the groom helped her into the saddle.

As soon as she and Princess Amalie were mounted, Prince Stefan cantered off and they had to hurry to catch up with him.

He took them away from the Palace to where there was a long stretch of uncultivated land, which ran beside the river Latasha had seen when she arrived.

The moment he reached the river, Prince Stefan let his horse break into a gallop and they followed behind him.

To Latasha it was sheer delight to feel the stallion moving beneath her.

And to see a flood of yellow and mauve butterflies rising from the flowers in the grass.

She had read about all this in one of her books and it was a thrill to see it actually happening before her eyes.

Well ahead of them, Prince Stefan galloped on for nearly twenty minutes.

Then as his horse slowed down they caught up with him.

"That was incredibly wonderful!" Latasha cried out enthusiastically.

"I thought that you would enjoy yourself," Prince Stephan called to her. "I was told you were a very good rider and I take my hat off to you."

Latasha smiled at him.

"Thank you – that is the nicest compliment I could possibly receive."

"Do you like compliments?" he enquired. "I always thought the English did not appreciate them."

"I can assure you that we appreciate them as much as the women of any other nation."

"Then I must tell you that you ride brilliantly and we must undoubtedly have a race before you leave us."

"A race? What sort of race?"

"Before my brother was wounded we used to have races amongst our friends on a Racecourse which is on the other side of the Palace. Now no one bothers to arrange races and the Racecourse has been half forgotten."

"Oh, do let us have a race!" cried Latasha. "It will be very exciting. But I must have the opportunity to get to know your horses beforehand, as I would like to win and say it is a win for Great Britain!"

"You will have it," he promised her, "but actually Kraus could arrange it so much better than I can."

"How long has he been so ill?" Latasha asked him.

"I think it is nearly a year now. Of course, it was those Russians. Is it ever anything else? The only thing I can say is, let us enjoy ourselves while we can, because it is unlikely any of us will be here tomorrow."

"You must not think like that, Prince Stephan, you must make up your mind to fight them and to win!"

"It all depends on what we would have to do – "

As he spoke he put his horse into a gallop again.

Latasha guessed that he did not wish to discuss how they could stave off the Russians.

She did not blame him and it was obviously most unpleasant for a young man of twenty-three to be told he must marry someone selected for him by Queen Victoria.

Someone who might not even share in any of his interests, in particular riding.

'I am sorry for him,' Latasha said to herself as they galloped back the way they had come.

At the same time she knew that she had no wish to marry him.

CHAPTER FIVE

They arrived breathlessly back at the Palace.

As they were feeling hot after riding so fast, the two girls went at once upstairs to change.

They put on thin muslin dresses and hurried down to breakfast.

Latasha was just finishing her coffee when an *aide-de-camp* entered to inform her that the Head Gardener was waiting for her as she had requested.

She only kept him for a few minutes.

When she went outside she found he was an elderly man who had been at the Palace for many years and he was to her relief most knowledgeable on flowers and herbs.

"What I require from you," she said, speaking in his language, "is a plant which grows wild in England and is a common perennial herb."

She saw that he was listening and so she continued,

"It is a wild variety of chrysanthemum, but I do not know what it is called in this country. It has yellow-green leaves."

The Head Gardener murmured to himself the word 'chrysanthemum' several times –

"I thinks I knows what you mean, my Lady. Come with me."

He took her over several lawns bordered with huge flower beds ablaze with colour and then he opened an iron gate that led into what appeared to be an orchard.

There were many fruit trees in full blossom and the grass beneath them was bright with wild flowers.

Growing against one of the walls were the stems of what in England was called feverfew.

Latasha gave a cry of delight and she realised that the Head Gardener was surprised when she ran towards it.

"This is exactly what I want!" she cried. "This is what will cure His Royal Highness of his migraine."

She thought that the Head Gardener did not seem at all impressed, so she added,

"I assure you my mother has given it to hundreds of people who suffer from headaches and migraine and they have all been cured."

She then started to look for the smallest leaves that were just beginning to sprout.

The air was very warm in this part of the world, she thought, and the plants that did not appear until the autumn in England would now just be coming into flower.

She was not mistaken.

The leaves of the feverfew were peeping from the stems.

She found six feverfew plants, plucked a handful of leaves from them and told the Head Gardener,

"I promise you that His Royal Highness will benefit from these leaves and therefore it is essential that he should have them every day."

"We'll all do anything, my Lady, to help His Royal Highness back to health. I remembers him as a small boy, full of energy and stronger than any boy of his age and it's so sad for us to see him as he is now."

"If you now do what I tell you," explained Latasha, "he will be a different man in a very short time."

Carrying the small leaves in her hand she started to walk back to the Palace accompanied by the Head Gardner.

As they stepped into the garden, Latasha looked up at the trees.

Many were trees she had seldom seen in England.

Then she gave a loud exclamation,

"What is that tree?" she asked the Head Gardner.

It was a large old-looking tree and its bright green leaves were strangely shaped. They were almost like small fans or an ornamentation to a woman's gown.

The Head Gardener smiled at her.

"That be a tree that were brought here from China many years ago by His Royal Highness's grandfather."

"China!" cried Latasha.

"He were a most enthusiastic traveller and brought back many rare plants. Orchids were indeed his particular favourite, but also there were one or two strange trees just like that one."

"Do you know what it is called?"

The Head Gardener smiled.

"Ginkgo Biloba, and I have often laughed at a tree having such a strange name."

"I have heard of it and it is in fact a very wonderful tree. In ancient China it was used in temples and shrines and therefore considered almost holy."

"Well, I never hears that before, my Lady, but one lives and learns."

"What is important," Latasha went on, "is that the leaves have great healing power. They give those who eat them strength and they live very much longer than is usual for human beings."

"Well I never did," the Head Gardener muttered. "I

always thought it were a pretty tree, but I wasn't told all them things about it."

"Now what we need immediately are the youngest leaves which must be given to the chef every day. Also the seed which has a waxy bloom the colour of silver apricot."

The Head Gardener stared at her in astonishment.

"Are you saying, my Lady," he enquired, "that His Royal Highness is going to eat the leaves of this tree *too*?"

"He is going to eat not only the leaves but also the seeds. The chef will incorporate them into his food so that he will hardly taste them, but he will reap the advantage by swallowing them."

The Head Gardener looked at her in sheer disbelief.

He obviously suspected she was talking nonsense or pulling his leg.

Then because he was impressed by the tree itself he thought maybe she was telling him something he had never come across before.

Latasha showed him the correct size of the young leaves she specially wanted and then told him to search for the pollen grains.

He promised he would do it himself and not trust it to any of the under-gardeners.

"If it will really help His Royal Highness," he said, "then your Ladyship knows I'll do anything to help make him well."

"I remember hearing," Latasha told him, "that more that three hundred and fifty years ago in China the leaves were recognised as having such an amazing effect on the human body."

She sighed before she continued,

"My mother always longed for us to have a Ginkgo Biloba tree in our garden at home, but unfortunately we did not know anyone travelling to China who could bring one back home for us."

"This one here's grown larger and stronger since it arrived," the Head Gardener boasted proudly.

"Now it will perform the miracles I have heard it can do and its first one will be to make His Royal Highness as strong and healthy as he used to be."

She picked a few of the young leaves and instructed the Head Gardener to pick some more.

Then she ran back to the Palace.

She did not look for Princess Amalie, but went at once to His Royal Highness's apartments.

The *aide-de-camp* outside the room guarded by the sentries looked at her in surprise.

"I wish to see His Royal Highness immediately."

"His Royal Highness has not finished his breakfast, my Lady," the *aide-de-camp* replied. "And he never sees anyone so early."

"Tell him *please* that I have to see him and it is of the utmost importance," Latasha pleaded.

Reluctantly the *aide-de-camp* disappeared into the room.

Latasha waited impatiently outside the door, but did not have to wait long.

The *aide-de-camp* returned looking shocked.

"His Royal Highness will see you, my Lady, but he regrets that he is not yet dressed."

"That is not important."

The door was opened for her and Latasha walked straight in.

Prince Kraus was sitting in an armchair and on the table at his side was his breakfast.

He was wearing a red dressing-gown and there was a silk scarf around his neck.

He looked up as she came towards him and smiled.

"I understand, Lady Gloria, that you wish to see me urgently."

"Very urgently indeed, Your Royal Highness, for I have found two miraculous items in the garden, which will cure your aches and pains and make you well again."

"I only hope that is true, but I have to admit that I slept all night last night without waking."

"I will massage your head again in a few minutes," suggested Latasha, "but first you must allow me to tell you what I have just found in your garden."

She spoke excitedly.

Prince Kraus had an amused twinkle in his eyes as he encouraged her,

"Go ahead, please."

"First of all," she began, "Your Royal Highness has to eat these."

She held out her right hand on which there were six small leaves.

"What are they?" he questioned.

"They are called feverfew in England and they will cure your headaches and migraine almost at once, in fact if you take these every day as I have ordered from your Head Gardener, you will not be troubled any longer."

"I am just longing to believe you, Lady Gloria, but I find it hard to think that what you are saying can come true so quickly."

"I promise you that I am not exaggerating," Latasha insisted. "So please eat these before I tell you any more."

Prince Kraus took the small leaves from her and ate them one by one.

"They taste rather like lettuce leaves," he remarked.

"They have the power to cure you of your migraine which lettuce leaves do not have," retorted Latasha.

"Now what is next?" he asked, looking at the other leaves she was holding.

"I am just wondering, Your Royal Highness, how you could have a specimen of the oldest tree in the world, dating back for millions of years, in your garden without knowing it."

Prince Kraus stared at her.

"Which tree are you talking about?"

"The Ginkgo Biloba and I could hardly believe my eyes when I saw it, but its leaves, as you can see here, are different from any others. My mother has spoken of them so often and their amazing properties."

He was still staring at her.

"I know which tree you mean now. My grandfather brought it back with him from China. It has grown well in our garden, but we never thought it was of any particular significance."

"Nor did your Head Gardener, but I told him that it was grown in ancient Chinese temples and shrines. It not only appeared in their literature for the very first time in the eleventh century but also in their paintings."

"This is certainly a great surprise to me. But why is it particularly important?"

"Because of its wonderful healing qualities. The Chinese believed it would make those who took it strong in body and brain."

Prince Kraus gave a little laugh.

"This is really growing in my garden and I had no idea of it?"

"Your Royal Highness should be eternally grateful to your dear grandfather. My mother always knew that the leaves from the Ginkgo Biloba help to carry the blood all over the body reaching the hands, feet and the heart."

"So after all these many thousands of years I am to consume the Ginkgo Biloba tree?"

"You may be laughing at the idea at this moment," answered Latasha, "but you will soon be grateful for what it will do for you. That is why I want you to send now for your chef and let me explain to him what you will require every day in your food."

She spoke firmly as if she was giving an order.

Then she realised that his eyes were twinkling at her again.

She looked at him and laughed.

"It is all right. I know I am behaving like a very bossy nanny. But you have to get well. It is ridiculous at your age not to be able to do all the things that men like your friend the Duke can do."

"You are right," he agreed. "When I think of Harry taking those huge jumps he always enjoys, I am furious I can no longer do it myself."

"If you do what I ask of you," Latasha said quietly, "I promise that in a few days you will feel the difference and in a few weeks you too will be jumping on one of your magnificent stallions I have just been riding."

"Do you swear to me, Lady Gloria, that this is not just some pie in the sky and I will not wake up to find I am feeling even worse than I have felt before?"

"I think if you are honest you will admit that you feel so much better this morning, because you have slept so well without waking in the night."

"That is indeed true," Prince Kraus agreed.

"Well you have to trust me, Your Royal Highness. You let me massage the pain away last night and I want to massage your head again this morning before you start the day. But first we must speak to your chef."

Prince Kraus laughed.

"I can see, Lady Gloria, that you are used to getting your own way!"

"Only when it concerns those who cannot look after themselves."

"And you think that is something I cannot do?"

"Not at the moment," she answered, "and if there is anything I hate it is to see a strong man struck down by illness when he can be easily cured by herbs and the many other amazing products of nature."

She was speaking seriously and once again she saw Prince Kraus's eyes were twinkling.

"You are far too young and too beautiful to worry about other people. Why are you not, like most women do, thinking about yourself?"

"I suppose it is all my mother's fault for having a famous herb garden, and for letting me help her to heal the people who came to visit her when every doctor had failed. They all went away well and happy because she knew what they really needed."

"Then I can only state that I am very grateful you have come here to Oldessa. If you can make me a complete man again, I will lay all my Kingdom at your feet."

"I might," replied Latasha, "ask you for one of your magnificent horses, but only if you are well enough to race me in the same way I was racing with Prince Stefan a little while ago."

"That is indeed a challenge, Lady Gloria."

As he spoke, he rang the bell by his side.

The door opened immediately and when an *aide-de-camp* appeared, he ordered,

"Tell the Head Chef I wish to speak to him now."

The *aide-de-camp* bowed and withdrew, looking at Latasha again with surprise in his eyes.

It was quite obvious he had not expected that Prince Kraus would have been willing to see her at such an early hour and he was surely even more surprised that after some considerable time had passed she was still there.

The Head Chef was a man of about thirty.

Latasha had already learnt that he had been trained in France.

"He has some French blood in him," Prince Kraus explained, "and when I realised how ambitious he was to produce new dishes, I sent him off to do a year's training under one of the most famous chefs in Paris."

"My father said the best food in the world comes from France," said Latasha, "and he always insisted we had a Frenchman in charge of the kitchen at home."

As she was speaking, she was afraid that she might have made a blunder.

He might remember that this was true of his friend Harry's house as he had stayed there when they were both at Oxford.

Fortunately however the Head Chef came in at that precise moment.

The Prince explained to him Lady Gloria's delight in finding there was a Ginkgo Biloba tree in the garden.

The Head Chef listened attentively.

Latasha appreciated that he was not like many chefs who were so puffed up with their own importance that they did not want to learn anything new.

She told him, as she had told Prince Kraus, of the Ginkgo Biloba's reputation in China.

She showed him the leaves and he agreed it would be easy to incorporate them and the seeds in food without anyone being aware of it.

He would also mix them into a salad for the Prince to consume.

"It is difficult, my Lady," he sighed, "because His Royal Highness is eating very little at the moment. I try to tempt him with dishes that have a very delicious flavour to them."

"I thought you would do so anyway, but I think you will find that His Royal Highness will be enjoying his food very shortly."

She gave the Head Chef the leaves she had picked from the Ginkgo Biloba tree and told him that the Head Gardener would make sure he was supplied with as many leaves as he could use.

"I do not need to tell you," she then insisted, "that it is always important when using herbs to prevent pain or increase the nutrition in food, that they should be as fresh as possible."

"I understand, my Lady," he replied. "I can assure you everything that comes into my kitchen is as fresh as it is humanly possible to find."

"One more requirement, His Royal Highness is to eat two extra large spoonfuls of honey every morning and evening."

"I will get as fat as a pig!" he expostulated.

"You can well afford to put on at least two stone," commented Latasha.

"Our Oldessan honey is especially good," the Head Chef came in. "His Royal Highness will surely enjoy the sweetness of it."

"What more can you ask?" enquired Latasha.

She was laughing and Prince Kraus laughed too.

"I give in," he exclaimed. "Nanny always knows best!"

"I will prove it to you in two weeks."

"That *is* a challenge!"

"It may cost you a horse," Latasha reminded him.

"Or something even more precious – "

She wondered what Prince Kraus meant.

The Head Chef was looking a little uneasy during this exchange.

"I am much looking forward to luncheon today," Latasha now said to him, "and I would like to tell you how much I enjoyed your delicious dishes last night at dinner."

Obviously delighted with her compliment, the Head Chef bowed his way to the door.

Latasha looked at Prince Kraus.

"Would you like me to massage your head now, Your Royal Highness" she asked, "or have you had enough of me?"

"You know it would be quite impossible for me to say anything but how grateful I am for the trouble you are taking over me, Lady Gloria. Although my head is not aching, I would like my brain to be made a little clearer than it is at present."

Latasha rose and walked behind his chair.

He lent back and she then placed her fingers gently on his forehead, as she had done last night.

Then she began to move them slowly but firmly.

As she did so, she felt a strange feeling rise within herself – something she had never felt before.

She did not understand what it was or why it was there.

She only knew that she wanted with all her heart to make Prince Kraus strong and well again as he must have been when he and Harry were so happy together all those years ago.

"You are not to send me to sleep," he admonished her a few minutes later.

"I will try not to, but last night you were very tired and in pain and it was better to make you unconscious."

"I found it very difficult to believe, when I awoke this morning, that I had not moved from where you left me. I would like to believe that you were watching over me all night – "

Latasha gave a little laugh.

"Your Guardian Angel does that job for you. I am quite certain that it is why I am here and I have been sent from Heaven to save you from yourself."

She was speaking lightly, but the Prince remarked seriously,

"You are right. *Only* God knows what will happen to our country in the future if I cannot save it."

"I am sure you will do so. It is something you must believe in, just as you believe that what I am doing to you will make you well."

"That is easy, Lady Gloria. I do believe in you and I trust you. May I say you are different from anyone else I have ever met in my whole life?"

Latasha did not answer.

She merely continued to massage his head for about a further ten minutes.

Then she said,

"I am sure that you will find it easier to think more clearly, especially as the feverfew will now be working."

"My head does feel lighter and clearer than it has for a long time. When will you come and see me again?"

"I am going to give your sister an English lesson while we are exploring the Palace. But I know we would both enjoy having luncheon with you, if that is possible."

Prince Kraus smiled.

"I will make it possible. So I will expect you both at one o'clock."

Latasha smiled back at him, dropped him a graceful curtsy and then left the room.

She was aware without looking back that his eyes were following her until she had passed through the door.

As the *aide-de-camp* stared at her as if waiting for an explanation, she hurried away to find Princess Amalie.

The girl was only too willing to take Latasha round the Palace.

They inspected all the pictures, the china and the wonderful collection of antique snuffboxes.

Amalie learnt the English word for everything they admired.

Eventually they came to the library which was large and impressive.

Latasha gave a cry of delight.

"Look at all these marvellous books! I only wish I had time to read them all."

"You will find some of them very dull," Princess Amalie remarked.

"But most of them very intriguing," added Latasha.

She took a book on Greece from one of the shelves and showed Amalie illustrations of the Goddesses and the Greek temples.

"That one is just like you," Amalie said pointing to a picture of Aphrodite.

"The Goddess of Love! I only wish it was true."

"You are so pretty. There must be heaps of men in love with you."

"What I am really looking for, Amalie, and what you too must look for, is the one man who will love you with all his heart and soul. You will love him too in the same way. That is what makes a happy marriage."

"But I am Royal and I will have to marry someone who will be a help to my country."

"I do know that, Amalie, but at the same time some arranged marriages can be very happy."

"When Kraus told Stefan that he had to marry an English bride, he was very angry. He said he did not want to marry anyone."

"I would undoubtedly expect that one day he will change his mind," mused Latasha.

Amalie thought for a moment and then she said,

"I do think Stefan would like to know lots of pretty ladies before he then 'settles down', as Kraus calls it, with a wife and family."

Latasha knew this to be very true, but she thought it a mistake to say much to Amalie.

The girl was obviously intelligent enough to realise what was happening in Oldessa, but before she could say anything more Amalie went on,

"Do you really think that, if Stefan will not marry an English Princess, the Russians will come in and turn us out of the Palace?"

There was unmistakeable fear in Amalie's eyes.

Latasha answered her quickly,

"I am sure nothing like that will ever happen."

"But if Stefan says 'no' to the Queen of England, then she will not protect us against the Russians – "

Latasha thought it was unfortunate that she should be troubled by this particular question, but it was no use telling Amalie it was all untrue if she had already heard her two brothers discussing the problem.

Maybe they had both been unaware that she was listening to them.

"Let us go and look at the Picture Gallery," Latasha suggested hastily, "but then I must return to the library to find some more books to read."

Amalie gave a little cry.

"There is a book here, which you will like because it is in English and it is all about your friend."

Amalie climbed up to take a book from one of the higher shelves.

"Kraus brought this little book back from England and told me it was about the people he had stayed with. It was the first time I had seen a family tree that is as old as ours."

Amalie brought the book she was talking about to Latasha.

She saw at a quick glance that it was the history of the Norlingtons. Harry must have given it to Prince Kraus as soon as it was republished.

That had been immediately after their father died and he became the Duke.

She took the book from Amalie saying,

"How kind of you to show it to me and I will enjoy reading it. Now we must find a book for you and of course it must be in English."

"I would like a fairy story," admitted Amalie. "My last Governess said I was too old for them, but I do like the fairy stories so much."

"So do I, Amalie, and I am sure there must be one here somewhere."

They looked along the shelves and found a very old edition of *Grimm's Fairy Tales*.

Latasha carried it up the stairs to the sitting room she was sharing with Amalie.

They were just sitting down together to read from the book when Prince Stefan came in.

"I would like to talk to you now, Lady Gloria. Run along, Amalie, and play in the garden until I call for you."

His sister got up reluctantly, putting the book down.

"I am in the middle of one of my English lessons, Stefan, and you should not interrupt us."

"I will not keep Lady Gloria for very long and your English is already improving."

Amalie smiled at him.

"I am going to make it as good as yours and then you will not be able to laugh at me."

She ran out of the room.

Latasha looked enquiringly at Prince Stefan.

"What is it? What has happened," she asked him apprehensively.

"I have just read a disturbing report from one of our Generals who did not wish to worry my brother."

"What sort of report?" enquired Latasha.

"He thinks the Russians are now paying particular attention to Oldessa, as we are so prosperous compared to the other Principalities in this area of the Balkans. They will therefore make every effort to take over our country."

Latasha chose her words carefully as she replied,

"The Duke of Norlington told me before I came out here that you were worried. He asked me when I returned to report to him about the situation as I saw it."

"Well you can tell him we are all frightened, but I daresay Norlington told you that if I married a relation of Queen Victoria, we would be safe."

"I think that scenario would equally apply to quite a number of Principalities," commented Latasha evasively.

"What I am asking you, is what I can do about this situation. I have no wish to marry some English girl I have never seen, who will doubtless be very unattractive."

As he spoke he remembered that Lady Gloria was English and what he had said was therefore rather rude.

"What I really mean," he added quickly, "is that if she is as beautiful as you are, she would have been snapped up already and would not then want some obscure Balkan Prince as a husband."

Latasha laughed.

"You are making it sound very unattractive. I am sure the marriages Her Majesty has arranged in other parts of the Balkans and Germany have on the whole been pretty happy."

"That is just what they *have* to say," replied Prince Stephan. "If you ask me they make the best of a bad job. But that is not my business. What I am concerned with is myself and at the moment I do not wish to marry anyone."

"I can quite understand. But you have to think of your country."

"That is Kraus's business as long as he is alive. I am just asking you how I can get out of being tied up to an English wife when I want to be free."

"It is, of course," said Latasha, "a decision I cannot make. When I return to England I will tell the Duke what you feel and perhaps he can think of a better way of saving your country."

"I do not mean to be rude, Lady Gloria, but might I ask when you are leaving?"

"I think after what you have just told me, it will be perhaps at the end of this week or early next week. I only came on a short visit anyway."

Prince Stephan smiled at her.

"It is most decent of you to take any trouble over me, but to tell the truth I want to enjoy myself while I am still young and lively. A jealous wife would undoubtedly be an encumbrance."

Latasha laughed again.

"That much is true at any rate!"

He glanced towards the door.

"Please, *please*, help me," he urged her in a low voice. "They are all pushing me, the Lord Chamberlain, all my relatives including Kraus, to send a petition to Queen Victoria."

Latasha thought for a moment.

"Don't do anything for just a few days. Let us both have time to think. If they keep worrying you, tell them to talk to me."

She paused for a moment before she added,

"I at least know what is happening in England and I can tell you one thing and that is that Queen Victoria is finding it very difficult to find enough brides for the heavy demands from the Balkans and elsewhere."

Prince Stefan looked surprised but he did not speak.

"What would be a grave mistake," Latasha went on, "would be for the Russians to know your petition had been refused by Queen Victoria, then there would be nothing to prevent them from walking into this country and taking it over."

Prince Stefan stared at her.

"I understand what you are saying and of course you are right. I will do whatever you say and play for time. But, of course, I am worried about Oldessa just as Kraus is. It is our country and why should we allow the Russians to take control of it?"

"Why indeed? It is what they have already done to a number of other countries and there is nothing to prevent them from doing it again unless our Queen Victoria stands in their way."

Prince Stephan made a helpless gesture.

"You make it sound as if I am doomed – "

"Just do what I say and wait and see. Miracles can happen when we least expect them and all we can do at the moment is to pray for a miracle."

He sighed.

"You are being incredibly decent about this, Lady Gloria, and I am very grateful."

"All I am doing at this very moment is trying to make your brother strong and healthy again."

"I am afraid it is impossible. The doctors have told me that there is nothing more they can do."

Latasha smiled.

"Please just wait and see. I always enjoy proving that the doctors are invariably wrong."

"I hope you can do so. They are always the same. When things go right they take all the credit, but when it all goes wrong they just say it is an act of God and there is nothing they can do about it."

"Well, I will try very hard to prove them wrong, but you must give me a little time in which to do so."

Prince Stephan walked towards the door.

"Do come for another ride with me after luncheon, Lady Gloria. The one thing which takes my mind off all this trouble and misery is a very fast horse."

"I agree with you, and I am sure Amalie would love to ride with you again."

He smiled at her and waved his hand.

Then he disappeared.

Latasha walked to the window.

She could see Amalie sitting in the garden by the fountain.

She thought how peaceful everything looked.

And how beautiful all the flowers, the birds and the sunshine were.

Was it possible that the Russians might walk in at any moment and destroy everything?

The idea had seemed unreal in England and even here it seemed most unlikely.

'I just don't believe it and I don't want to believe it,' Latasha said to herself.

At the same time there was a large looming cloud of darkness somewhere out there on the horizon that might easily envelop the sun.

CHAPTER SIX

Latasha and Amalie went out shopping in the City.

She chose Amalie some very pretty dresses which were nearer to grown-up in design than those she had been used to wearing.

She also bought a dress for herself.

The Proprietor bowed them respectfully to the door.

"I hope you are doing well here," Latasha remarked as they waited for the carriage to be brought round.

"Not as well as we have been doing," the Proprietor replied.

Latasha looked surprised.

"Why ever not?"

His voice lowered as he came a little nearer to her,

"People are worried as to what is going to happen to Oldessa. A number of our distinguished families are thinking of moving out of the country and in the meantime they are not making many purchases."

"I am sorry to hear that, but I am sure your fears are unfounded."

As she was speaking to him their carriage came to a standstill opposite them.

She and Amalie climbed into the carriage.

As they drove off, Amalie asked Latasha,

"Did he mean that the people are frightened of the Russians?"

"Yes, that is what he meant, but I think the whole scare is being exaggerated."

"Many of the Palace servants are terrified."

Latasha knew this was true as Nanny had told her that they were in a complete panic below stairs – they kept wondering what would happen to them if the Russians took over.

"Prince Stephan's valet is so sure," Nanny had told her, "that they'd compel His Royal Highness to obey their orders and to run the country under their thumb. But the Head Chef and some of the other men thinks they'd turn the Royal Family out altogether."

Latasha did not answer Nanny.

She was waiting for a letter from Harry to tell her what was happening in England.

She had not yet written him a report because it was difficult to know exactly what to say.

It would be no use just informing him that Prince Stefan did not wish to be married and especially not to an English girl.

They drove off.

Some people recognised the carriage and waved to Princess Amalie.

Latasha suggested that she should wave back and she looked surprised.

"My Governesses always told me that I was not to notice the ordinary people, but to look straight ahead."

"They must all have been very silly women. These are your people and they want to be friendly because they are so fond of you. Of course you must wave to them and be careful not to ignore anyone."

"That sounds much more fun!" exclaimed Amalie.

She almost lent out of the carriage to wave to some children they were passing.

As they drove on, the flowers were more beautiful than ever and so were the trees in blossom.

It was such a lovely country from what Latasha had already seen of it and it seemed so cruel that they should be terrorised by the Russians or anyone else.

They arrived back at the Palace.

To her delight when they entered the hall one of the footmen handed her a letter on a silver tray.

She saw at once that it was from Harry.

So she hurried upstairs so that she could read it in the quiet of her bedroom.

As she opened it she thought he would reproach her for not having written to him.

Instead he began his letter,

"Dearest Latasha,

Wonderful news and I know you will be delighted.

Her Majesty the Queen sent for me yesterday and I drove to Windsor Castle rather nervously fearing that she had something to say about you.

But I was mistaken.

When I arrived Her Majesty asked me if I would be Master of the Horse now that old Drummond has retired.

As you can imagine I jumped at the idea.

Of course it means I will have to spend more time in London. But it will be worth it to be able to clean up the Royal Stables and buy a great number of better horses than they possess at the moment."

Latasha turned over the page.

She was thinking that this was undoubtedly the best thing that could possibly happen to Harry.

If he went to live in London, he would meet many more people than he saw at the moment.

She had always hoped that sooner or later he would meet someone beautiful with whom he would fall in love and she would make him as happy as her father and mother had been.

On the next page Harry wrote,

"I have been hoping to hear from you, but I suppose it is too early for you to make up your mind what you feel about Prince Stefan.

From all I have heard he is a bit of a lad with the girls, but I feel sure you could keep him in order."

Latasha considered that was very unlikely.

The letter continued,

"I have been looking everywhere for a Governess and when I was at Windsor Castle I asked Lady Littleworth and the Countess of Selford if they knew of anyone.

The latter thought that she knew of a young woman who would definitely fit the post.

She said she would get in touch with her and let me know if she would be willing to go to Oldessa.

I have been doing what I can about this issue and I hope you will be pleased with me.

So much love, my dearest Latasha, and come home soon. I find it very lonely without you.

Your affectionate brother, Harry"

Latasha put the letter back in the envelope and hid it in her jewel case.

She wondered what she could possibly say to her brother about her situation.

She thought the best answer should be that Prince Stefan had no wish for a British bride and so it was up to him and his brother to keep the Russians from intruding by some other means.

She had no idea what it could be, but she reckoned that even Queen Victoria would find it hard to press a wife onto Prince Stefan.

She was tidying her hair when Nanny came into the room.

"I've just heard," she announced breathlessly, "that His Royal Highness intends to go riding tomorrow!"

Latasha gave a little cry.

"It's too early! He is not strong enough yet."

"His valet says as he's a different man since you've been treating him. If you've done nothing else for this here country, then they should be down on their knees for what you've done for their Prince."

"I doubt if they will," said Latasha with an amused smile. "At the same time I am so delighted that Mama's remedies have worked so splendidly. I do hope she knows that I have found a Ginkgo Biloba tree here."

"I'm sure her knows. Perhaps it was your mother and father who sent you here to help the poor Prince. It made me heart ache, it did, to hear how he's suffered while the doctors, as we might have guessed, were all helplessly wringing their hands and saying they couldn't prevent him from dying."

"Well, he's not going to die now, but I will not have him doing anything which will set back my treatment."

She walked out of the room as she spoke.

Nanny looked after her with a smile.

'She's very like her mother,' she sighed to herself. 'Eventually she always gets her own way!'

Latasha ran down the stairs and along the passage to the Royal Apartments.

The sentries knew her very well by now and saluted whenever she appeared.

The daily *aide-de-camp* in charge dutifully opened the door without being asked.

When she went in she found Prince Kraus sitting at his writing desk.

He looked up as she appeared and she said quickly,

"Please don't rise, you must still take things easy, Your Royal Highness. I hear, although I cannot believe it is true, that you are talking of riding tomorrow."

"I thought you would be pleased to have me as your companion, Lady Gloria, when you and Amalie go out in the morning before breakfast."

"Of course you must not – when you do go riding I will give you a special massage first and you must take it very easy the first time you mount a horse."

Prince Kraus lent back in his chair.

"I knew you would try to stop me, so when can I start?"

"Perhaps in two days time."

"I am not going to wait as long as that. I feel so much better in myself and I have not had a headache since you came to Oldessa. I must take some exercise, otherwise I will end up in a wheelchair!"

Latasha giggled.

"That is not likely, Your Royal Highness, looking as you do now. But I am so very worried that you might have a relapse and I will have to start at square one all over again."

"Would you mind having to do so?"

There was a pause before Latasha replied,

"I will have to return home sometime."

"I appreciate that, and I am also extremely curious to know what your report will be on Stefan."

Latasha stared at him wide-eyed.

"What can you mean?" she asked incredulously.

Prince Kraus smiled.

"I am not a complete idiot. I soon realised you had come here to spy out the land – for Harry."

Latasha drew in her breath.

She had no idea that he could be aware of the real reason why she was visiting him.

"When I wrote to Harry suggesting that his sister Latasha should marry Stefan, I thought perhaps he might suggest coming himself to pay me a visit. But when you appeared as his friend who was interested in travelling, I guessed exactly why he had sent you."

"As a spy?" she murmured.

"As a very charming, very clever and very beautiful spy! Which of course all women spies are traditionally!"

Latasha laughed.

"I don't think it is a compliment when you call me a spy. I will admit Harry asked me to let him know what I thought about Oldessa and I have every intention of telling him how lovely I think it is."

"And Stefan?" Prince Kraus enquired.

Latasha made a helpless gesture with her hands.

"He is determined to marry no one."

"That is exactly what he has said to me. Actually we had a flaming row about it last night."

"After you had had your massage, you should have gone to sleep," Latasha reproved him. "It is very wrong and naughty of Stefan and something I will not allow him to do again."

"You really think you can stop him?" Prince Kraus enquired. "He came up to say goodnight and when I asked him to accept a British bride to save Oldessa, he flew into a rage. He said that he was not going to be bullied by me or anyone else into marrying a plain, boring, stupid English girl!"

"Latasha is none of those things," she muttered to him indignantly.

"Surely, but because I told Stefan I thought he was selfish and unpatriotic, he and Madame le Telbé have gone off today to the Summer Palace."

Latasha's eyes widened.

"I did not know you had one."

"It is some miles away just over the mountains and was built by my father on the side of a lake. The situation is amazingly beautiful and the Palace although not very big is comfortable. Stefan will doubtless enjoy himself there."

"And you let him go?" Latasha said reproachfully.

Prince Kraus sighed expressively.

"What was the point of trying to stop him? He is over twenty-one and can now do what he likes. Personally I am a little tired of Madame le Telbé's endless silly giggles and flirtatious eyes. I thought it would be a nice rest without her!"

Latasha felt the same but knew she must not say so.

Instead she suggested,

"If I let you ride tomorrow, will you promise to do it no more than for only one hour in the morning and then lie down after luncheon?"

"I will ride with you at ten o'clock. We will have luncheon together when we return, but I make no promises as to what I will do in the afternoon."

"Now I know you are better, Your Royal Highness! When a patient starts defying his nurse, it means that he is really well again and has no further need of her."

"That is not true, Lady Gloria, I have great need of you, and what I want to do, as soon as that tiresome nurse of whom you are speaking allows me, is to show you some of the improvements I have introduced to Oldessa – "

He paused before he added,

"Also a discovery which has just been made in the mountains."

"A new discovery?" she asked excitedly. "What is it?"

"For the moment it must be a secret. I understand that those who are working in that particular area have all sworn on the Bible that they will keep silent about what they have found."

"And what have they found?"

Prince Kraus looked towards the door as if he felt that someone might be listening.

Then he said in a low voice only she could hear,

"*Gold*!"

Latasha gave a cry of delight.

"Gold! Surely that is most unusual."

"Very unusual, even for those in the Balkans who have lead, iron and coal. I don't think we have much gold, but even a little will cause a major sensation and make us outstanding amongst all the other countries around us."

"Of course it will," Latasha agreed, "and I am very pleased for you and Oldessa."

"And you will help me?"

"As much as I can, but I do not quite see how."

"I will tell you later, Lady Gloria, but first I want to show you and I want to see myself exactly what has been found in the mountains."

"It is so exciting," Latasha exclaimed. "I presume you have not yet told your brother."

"Certainly not, if I told Stefan, he would surely tell Madame le Telbé and what woman could possibly keep a secret like that?"

"But you have told *me*!"

"*You* are different."

"Why?" she asked him wide-eyed.

There was silence until Prince Kraus replied,

"Because you are so unlike in every way anyone I have ever met in my entire life."

He paused for a moment.

"Who else could have healed me when I thought I was facing death? Now I am determined to live if only to prove you are right."

Latasha clapped her hands together.

"That is exactly what I want you to say. But please, please do not run before you can walk. Mama was always insistent that people should get well slowly."

"The extraordinary thing is – I am *now* well. I am well in myself and I am sure the honey you have given me has already put on the first of the two stone you insist on my gaining."

Latasha smiled at him

"Your clothes still look a little loose on you."

"I certainly have no intention of being extravagant and buying others if I can only wear them for a short time."

They were both laughing and Latasha added,

"I think you have been doing exercises when I have not been looking!"

"I remembered those I learnt at school and I found I could not only do them very easily but they were definitely making my limbs move quicker and feel stronger than they have felt for a long time."

"I think really we have to thank the Ginkgo Biloba tree, Your Royal Highness. When I tell them at home that you have one growing in your garden, I feel they will be very jealous."

"Now to return to where we came in, Lady Gloria, "what reports have you given to the Duke?"

"None so far. Actually I had a letter from him this morning after shopping and it is good news for you."

"In what way?" Prince Kraus enquired.

"First of all the Duke has been appointed Master of the Horse by Her Majesty – "

"That will please Harry and he is exactly the right man to be Master of the Horse. What else did he say?"

"He said that whilst he was at Windsor Castle, he spoke to two distinguished ladies and one of them seems to know exactly the right Governess for Princess Amalie."

There was silence for a moment before he spoke,

"I am sure Amalie would much rather have you."

"I need to return to England very soon, Your Royal Highness."

"Why, is there some attractive young Englishman waiting for you?"

Latasha did not answer him and after a moment, he added,

"I am now waiting to know if you are in love and engaged to be married."

"I do not want to answer questions about myself," she answered. "I came here because I wanted to visit the Balkans and I thought it would be amusing to stay in your Palace, while the Duke at your own request is looking for a Governess, and teach your sister English myself for a short while."

"Which you have certainly done extremely well. I was thinking only yesterday how fluent she had become. And she enjoys being with you, as indeed *I* do."

As he finished speaking their eyes met and Latasha felt a little tremor course through her body.

Then she told herself that she had come to prevent Prince Kraus from doing too much.

Now he should be resting.

So she rose to her feet.

"I am going into the garden and I think you should close your eyes and if possible sleep. Would you like me to massage your forehead now?"

He shook his head.

"Not at the moment," he replied, "and if you want to go into the garden, I will come too."

"Are you quite sure that it will not be too much for you, Your Royal Highness?"

He shook his head again.

"The only thing I am having far too much of at the moment is my own company. Because I am frightened of losing you, I want to keep you fully in sight of my eyes."

Latasha walked to the door and he followed her.

She had a feeling that he was holding onto her.

He was placing scores of invisible bands round her body to prevent her from flying away from him.

'He is apprehensive that if I leave,' she mused, 'he will fall sick again and there will be no one here to make him well.'

They walked out of the Palace by a side door and Latasha realised that Prince Kraus was now walking quite easily.

He was not dragging his legs as he had done when she had first arrived and it was obvious that his head was clear of headaches and migraine.

When he looked up at the sun, the light seemed to sparkle in his eyes.

He was so handsome silhouetted against the trees and was so different from any other man she had ever met.

Impulsively Latasha cried,

"*You are well*, you are really well! I can see it in your face and the way you move. All you have to do now is to be extremely careful. Then you will be as strong as you were when you were at Oxford with the Duke."

"I intend to be even stronger than that. When I was a small boy I enjoyed life wildly and passionately without thinking about it. Now I need to think clearly and what you will have to concentrate on, my beautiful nurse, is my brain."

"What can be wrong with your brain?"

"I have at the moment a problem I cannot solve and which is vital for both me and my country. There must be a way that I have not yet found of tackling and solving it."

Latasha did not understand what he was saying.

She guessed that it must in some way concern the menace of Russia.

Then she remembered that the real reason she was here in Oldessa was to take a good look at Prince Stefan to decide whether she would marry him as Prince Kraus had suggested to her brother.

Alternatively to take a chance that Queen Victoria would not recall her existence.

Other Royalty in deep need of a British wife might be different in every way to Prince Stefan.

They might be old, ugly and repulsive!

"Now you are looking worried," he interrupted her thoughts unexpectedly. "What have I said to disturb you?"

"I was just thinking of you and your problem, Your Royal Highness, but you must forget it for now and come and look at the Ginkgo Biloba tree. I think that you should bow respectfully to it and thank it for making you feel as you now do!"

He chuckled.

"Where is the tree? I seem to have forgotten."

Latasha put out her hand to guide him to where the Ginkgo Biloba tree stood.

As his fingers closed over hers, she felt again that strange feeling she had felt earlier in his presence.

Then, as they were walking together in the garden in silence, she became suddenly aware that she had fallen in love.

When they found the tree they both paid elaborate homage to it, which made them laugh.

They went back to the Palace and as they neared it, Amalie came running towards them.

She was wearing one of the new dresses they had just bought in the town and wanted her brother to admire it.

She told them that luncheon was ready and the chef was furious because they were late.

"I had totally forgotten all about luncheon," sighed Latasha.

"So had I," Prince Kraus admitted, "but now I think about it, I am feeling hungry."

"That is indeed good news," smiled Latasha.

"But I am worrying about my figure – "

"If you do not eat everything the chef has made for us, he will be cross or cry," came in Amalie. "He believes that your being so much better than you have been for a long time is all due to him."

"He must give a little credit to the Ginkgo Biloba tree!" replied Prince Kraus, his eyes twinkling.

"I am sure your chef thinks you should give him a medal when you are really well," said Amalie, "and he will be able to ask for a much bigger salary than he has now!"

"I am sure he has learnt a lot more in Paris than just cooking – the French have a clever way of extorting money from everyone when they least expect it!"

"That French woman has taken Stefan away from us," grumbled Amalie. "It is very mean of them to go off to the Summer Palace on their own and not ask us if we would like to go too."

"I think they just want to be alone. Personally I am perfectly content to be without them."

He looked at Latasha as he spoke, but she avoided his eyes.

As they entered the Palace, Amalie ran ahead to tell the butler she had found her brother and Lady Gloria.

They were all hungry and ready for their luncheon.

*

Later that afternoon Amalie was writing a story in English whilst Latasha went down to the library to find a book for herself.

She noticed that over the mantelpiece in the library there was a very striking portrait of Prince Kraus.

It had been painted over two years earlier and in it he was wearing the uniform of a General in the Oldessan Army.

His head was bare and the artist, who had obviously remarkable talent, had caught an expression of interest and enterprise in his eyes.

It made him seem as if he might just step out of the frame at any moment.

Latasha stood still gazing at the portrait.

She knew that she was right when she had admitted to herself that she was in love with Prince Kraus.

It was impossible not to love anyone so handsome.

She recognised that he had, now that he could use it effectively, such a quick brain that she had enjoyed every moment she had conversed with him.

She was in love as she had always wanted to be in love.

Then came the question which seemed to thunder in her ears – was he in love with *her*?

He paid her compliments and at the moment he said he could not be without her when she was making him well again.

But that was not the love she so desired.

She was well aware that perfect love really did exist if one could only find it.

He did admire her and she would not have been a woman if she could not have sensed it.

She had come into his apartment night after night to massage him and she had known by the way he watched her walking towards him that he thought she was beautiful.

But to Prince Kraus she was not Royal.

She was just an aristocratic English lady who had come to stay with him as a guest.

To save Oldessa, if his brother would not do it and now that his health was fully restored, he needed to marry Royalty.

Latasha had an agonising feeling deep within her.

Any Royal Englishwoman whatever she might look like would be more important to him at this very moment than anything he felt for her.

'How can I tell him who I am?' she asked herself. 'I

am sure that he would instantly offer me marriage. But if I don't, whatever he feels for me at the moment he would deem it impossible to offer me a wedding ring.'

To face the truth was like having a shower of iced water poured on something warm and lovely – something that was moving within her whenever she thought of him, looked at him or spoke to him.

'*I love him*,' she told herself again and again as she dressed for dinner.

She wore her prettiest gown, because she wanted to see the expression in his eyes.

'I really do love him,' she mused again, 'but what man, whoever he was, would sacrifice his country for his heart?'

Because she was allowed down to dinner, Amalie was in a wild state of excitement.

She came into Latasha's room to ask her if she was properly dressed.

"You look lovely, Amalie, and your brother will be very proud of you."

She was glad for the girl's sake when they walked downstairs and Prince Kraus, who was dining with them for the first time, announced,

"I am indeed flattered to have two such beautiful ladies with me. But now I am so much better we are going to have a great number of parties and you must listen to the compliments that you will receive from all the local Don Juans!"

Amalie giggled.

"I don't believe there are any. All the people who have come to luncheon here are old with white hair."

"I will find some young men for you," her brother promised.

"And what about some beautiful ladies for you?" Latasha asked of Prince Kraus a little mischievously.

"I have all I require at the moment," he replied to her firmly.

Then to Latasha's complete delight he began to tell them stories of what he had done when he was young and travelling the world.

He made them both laugh so that when dinner was over, Latasha thought it was the nicest meal she had ever had at the Palace.

Reluctantly, when it was time for them to move into the drawing room, Amalie had to go to bed.

"If you stay up too late," Latasha insisted, "you will be tired in the morning when we want to go riding before breakfast."

"And after breakfast you will be riding with me?" Prince Kraus interposed.

"Are you really riding so soon?" asked Latasha.

"I am, and no one is going to stop me. I have sent an order to the stables for the best mount so that you two will have to struggle hard to keep up with me!"

"Oh, please, please," Latasha begged him, "do take it slowly."

"I am *not* going to listen to you. Just for once I am going to do what I want to do. And that, I may say, will be a change!"

Latasha chuckled.

"The trouble with patients is they get spoilt because everyone makes too much fuss about them. Then they get uppish and, if they are not careful, they fall down before they reach the top!"

"Which is something I have no intention of doing, Lady Gloria, and when I do reach the very top on my own, it means that neither of you will be able to keep up with me and I shall expect a special prize from both of you."

"A special prize!" exclaimed Amalie. "I wonder what you want. It seems to me you have everything."

"Not everything," Prince Kraus muttered.

As he spoke his eyes met Latasha's.

It was impossible for either of them to look away.

When Amalie had gone to bed, they sat talking for nearly an hour.

"You must rest," persisted Latasha. "Please go and undress and I will come in a quarter-of-an-hour's time and massage you so that you will sleep peacefully all through the night."

"I would love it. Or else I will stay awake puzzling over the problem I have not yet solved – "

He did not wait for her to reply but walked from the room.

As the door closed behind him she wondered as she had wondered before what his problem was.

Could it possibly be what she had hoped – that he wanted her?

And yet he could see no possible way she could be his without putting his country in peril?

A little later she walked along the passages towards the Royal apartment.

She was feeling, although she tried to prevent it, a beautiful rapture moving inside her just because in a few moments she would be with him again.

'I am making a fool of myself,' she pondered. 'He does not love me in the same way.'

As she arrived at Prince Kraus's room the sentries came to attention.

An *aide-de-camp* opened the door for her.

"I am sure His Royal Highness is ready for you," he said as he bowed.

Latasha entered to find Prince Kraus was seated, as he always was, in his armchair.

His feet were raised and he had a soft rug over his knees.

He was undressed and wearing a dark robe with a silk scarf round his neck.

She walked towards him.

There was only one lamp left alight in the room and not until Latasha reached him did she realise he was asleep.

He was sleeping peacefully with a faint smile on his lips which told her he was happy.

She stood gazing at him for a long time, but had no reason to touch him.

She recognised that there would be little chance of his waking again before next morning – it was a healing sleep from natural exhaustion and not from weakness.

Finally as if she could not help herself Latasha went down on her knees.

She prayed as she had never prayed before that he would love her as she loved him.

She believed she was asking the impossible and yet God could perform miracles and that was what, at this very moment, she so needed more than anything in the whole world.

'I love him, I adore him,' she said in her heart.

And then her lips moved as she prayed again,

'Please God help me, please God give me his love!'

CHAPTER SEVEN

As they were planning to ride with Prince Kraus at eleven o'clock, Latasha decided that she and Amalie would not go out earlier.

She lay in bed later than usual, thinking.

Then she took breakfast with Amalie in their own sitting room.

"Do you really think that Kraus is well enough to ride today?" asked Amalie a little apprehensively.

"I am hoping so. I would like it to be two or three days later, but he is determined to prove himself well."

"He's certainly so very much better since you have been looking after him," said Amalie. "At one time I was scared that he was going to die."

"You need not be scared any more, Amalie. He is very definitely not going to die and in a short time you will all forget that he has even been so ill."

Amalie smiled happily.

As she got up from the table, she unexpectedly bent and kissed Latasha.

"You are *so* clever," she enthused. "I am very glad you came here to stay. Please don't go home *too* soon."

Latasha did not answer.

She had no wish to return to England.

At the same time she had the feeling that it would be wise for her to go.

She had put on her very best and prettiest habit for her ride with Prince Kraus.

When a little later she and Amalie went downstairs they saw through the open front door that the horses were outside and waiting for them.

Before she could ask the question one of the *aides-de-camp* announced,

"His Royal Highness is already mounted."

"We are not late!" Latasha exclaimed as if he had accused her.

"No, you are well on time, my Lady," the *aide-de-camp* replied.

They ran out to see that Prince Kraus was already mounted on a particularly fine and outstanding stallion.

Grooms were holding their horses for Latasha and Amalie.

Behind them Latasha noticed that there were two senior Officers already mounted – she knew these were the escort for Prince Kraus.

Prince Stefan was allowed to ride without one.

But as reigning Prince of Oldessa it was impossible for Prince Kraus to travel anywhere without an escort or a Guard of Honour.

Latasha quickly mounted her horse. It was one she knew well and had ridden before.

Then she trotted forward to join Prince Kraus who was waiting for her.

As she looked at him, she knew without being told that he was an exceptionally fine rider.

It was the way he sat on a horse.

As her father had once said,

"You must look part of the horse you are riding."

She guessed that Prince Kraus would be as good a rider as Harry.

They set off at a canter without talking with Prince Kraus leading the way.

As she followed him Latasha could not help feeling her heart was turning somersaults.

The sunshine was brighter than it had ever been.

'I love him, I love him,' she told herself again and again.

But she knew the real question was if he loved her in the same way.

It would be an intolerable agony to be his wife just because her blood was Royal.

She tried not to think about it at this moment, but found it impossible not to do so.

Prince Kraus now broke into a sharp gallop and her horse followed.

Latasha forgot everything else but the joy of riding through the thick grass.

Clouds of butterflies were rising in a kaleidoscope of colour in front of them.

They rode for what seemed a long time.

They were now well out of sight of the Palace and the houses of the City.

Prince Kraus drew his horse down to a walk and as Latasha came up beside him, he told her,

"Now I know that I am a man again. That gallop has done more for me than two bottles of champagne."

Latasha laughed.

"I hope, now you are better, you will not indulge in such a manner. It could be very bad for you."

"I am aware of that. I was only trying to explain

how elated I feel now I am back on a horse and no longer an invalid with people speaking to me in hushed voices."

Latasha laughed again.

Amalie caught up with them and called out,

"I am trying to ride faster than you, Kraus, but my horse is not as big as yours."

"I think you ride better than when I last saw you in the saddle."

His sister flushed with pleasure.

The two soldiers of the Royal Escort were keeping well behind and Latasha thought that was definitely on His Royal Highness's instructions.

Without thinking, as the thought had just came into her mind, she remarked,

"It must be a major bore always to have a Guard of Honour wherever you go, Your Royal Highness."

"There is one place where I manage to avoid it," he answered. "I will tell you about it later."

She wondered why there was a mystery about this place, but did not ask any questions.

They broke into a canter and almost as if she was giving the instructions and a short while later Prince Kraus turned back for home.

"You allowed me an hour, Lady Gloria, and today I am not going to play truant, although I make no promises for tomorrow!"

"The most important point is that you should not overtire yourself," Latasha stipulated firmly.

"At this very moment I feel so incredibly elated," he replied, "I would like to ride to the horizon and beyond it."

Latasha gave a cry of protest, but he added,

"However I am obeying orders, nurse, so you will have no reason to complain about me."

"I have never done so. You have been a very good patient because you have done what you were told."

She was speaking lightly.

Then as their eyes met, it was again very difficult to look away.

Amalie joined them and they rode on in silence.

As they reached the Palace, Latasha realised there were quite a number of people waiting to see them arrive.

She was sure it was not just curiosity as they must be worried in case the exercise had been too much for their Prince.

He waved in their direction, dismounted and patted his stallion's neck.

As the groom led him to the stables, Prince Kraus walked into the Palace.

When Latasha joined him a few seconds later, she counselled,

"I think that you ought to lie down now at least till luncheon time which we will make half-an-hour late."

"I will do so if it really pleases you," he responded unexpectedly. "But I would like to talk to you later in the afternoon alone."

The way Prince Kraus spoke made Latasha look at him enquiringly.

By this time they had reached the entrance into his apartments.

As the sentries came to attention, he walked in and the door closed behind him.

As she went to her room, Latasha was wondering what he wanted to talk to her about.

She realised that what she really wanted to hear him say was just impossible.

As she reached her own room, an idea shot through her mind.

Supposing, recognising that he could not marry her, Prince Kraus proposed something different?

It could be what the Comte had wanted to propose in the Orient Express.

The idea was startling and unexpected.

Latasha walked to the window.

Looking out below her, she did not see the beauty of the flowers, nor the water in the fountain shimmering in the sunshine.

Instead she could visualise the long years she might be forced to spend without him and without the miraculous rapture she now felt every time she looked at him.

Yet if he offered her what she suspected, it would mar and besmirch her love for him.

It would be impossible for her ever to feel the same about him again.

For quite a long time she stood blindly looking out of the window.

Then she heard Nanny come in behind her.

"Oh you're back, dearie!" she exclaimed. "I wasn't expecting you so soon."

"It was His Royal Highness's first day on a horse and it would be a mistake for him to ride for too long."

"I do agree with you," said Nanny, "but I saw him riding off and I thinks he's as good a rider as Master Harry – I mean His Grace."

Latasha gave a little laugh.

Nanny always forgot and called them by the names she used when they were children.

"Now what would you like to wear for luncheon?"

Nanny was saying. "I don't know if it's a party, but there's several dresses you've not worn yet."

Latasha let Nanny choose what she thought was the prettiest and then she sat down while she arranged her hair.

"I'll say one thing for you, dearie, you're looking much prettier since you've been here than you ever looked before. Maybe you're eating some of them Ginkgo Biloba leaves they're all talking about downstairs."

"We must try and get one from China to plant in our garden. I know it's a tree my mother always wanted."

"Well, it has certainly done wonders for His Royal Highness," said Nanny. "And as the Head Chef puts it into everyone's food they're all a-saying they be feeling better too."

She paused for a moment before adding,

"If I tells you the truth, I feel a year or two younger myself than I felt when I came here!"

"Oh, Nanny, that is marvellous! You must support me when we go home into making His Grace buy a Ginkgo Biloba for the herb garden."

"When are we to going home then, dearie?" Nanny asked her.

There was silence and then Latasha mumbled,

"Very soon – perhaps tomorrow."

If Prince Kraus said to her what she suspected he was about to say, she would leave at once.

She rose from off the stool in front of the dressing table.

As she did so the door burst open and Amalie came running in.

"*They are here*! They are here!" she cried out in a terrified voice. "I saw them when I went downstairs and I came straight back to tell you."

"Who are here?" demanded Latasha anxiously.

"The Russians! There are lots and lots of them and I saw them going into the Throne Room, so I know Kraus is in there talking to them."

Latasha stood very still and then she walked over to the secretaire in the corner of her bedroom.

She wrote something on a piece of paper.

Then she opened the drawer of the dressing table to take something out of her handbag.

Amalie was clinging to Nanny.

"They will hurt us, even *kill* us," she was howling.

"I don't think they will," Nanny told her quickly. "They're nasty people, there's no doubt about that, but I'm sure they won't touch you or her Ladyship."

She was speaking bravely, but Latasha knew by the tone of her voice that she too was feeling scared.

"Stay here with Nanny," Latasha told Amalie, "and don't be afraid. They will not hurt your brother or anyone else."

"How can you be sure?" asked Amalie. "They have done terribly cruel things to so many people. I have heard about it and read about it in the newspapers."

Now there were tears running down her cheeks.

Latasha picked up a book that was lying by her bed and said to Nanny,

"Look after the Princess. I promise you both that the Russians will not hurt you."

Nanny gave her a weak smile.

"I knows what you're up to, dearie, and God bless you."

Latasha did not answer, but walked quickly out of the bedroom and down the stairs.

As she passed by the front of the hall, she could see through the windows a large troop of Russian soldiers on horseback waiting outside.

She walked on towards the private apartments of His Royal Highness, Prince Kraus.

When she arrived, she found a number of *aides-de-camp* and elderly courtiers in an agitated group outside the Throne Room.

The Major-domo was standing guard firmly in the doorway obviously to prevent anyone from entering.

Latasha walked up to him and handed him the piece of paper on which she had written in her bedroom.

"Please announce me exactly as it is written here," she demanded firmly.

The Major-domo stared at her in astonishment.

"I don't think you can fully understand, my Lady," he gasped, "the Russians are here talking with His Royal Highness."

"I know," responded Latasha, "and the answer is in your hand."

The Major-domo was an elderly man and she had only seen him once or twice since her arrival at the Palace.

He looked down at the paper she had handed him.

Then he stiffened and without saying any more, he opened the door.

The Throne Room was large and imposing and at a glance Latasha could easily appreciate why Prince Kraus had decided to receive the Russians here.

The throne was in the centre of a low platform and Prince Kraus was sitting on it.

There were draped curtains behind him.

Beside Prince Kraus stood the Lord Chamberlain,

the Prime Minister and some Members of the Cabinet and three senior *aides-de-camp* were in attendance.

They were all facing the Russians.

There were about twelve stern-faced Russians and their leader was wearing a General's uniform covered with decorations.

He was speaking in a gruff guttural voice to Prince Kraus.

In a loud stentorian voice that seemed to echo all around the Throne Room, the Major-domo announced,

"Lady Latasha Ling, daughter of the fifth Duke of Norlington and Her Royal Highness Princess Beatrice of Saxe-Coburg, now requests an audience with Your Royal Highness."

As he finished speaking the Russian General turned round.

Everyone's eyes followed Latasha, as she moved slowly and deliberately across the Throne Room.

She walked up the steps that led onto the platform where Prince Kraus was sitting and went directly to him.

She did not curtsy as she had always done to him, but held out her hand.

Prince Kraus rose to his feet.

Although she did not look directly at him, she soon realised he was staring at her.

He took her hand and raised it to his lips.

Latasha turned round.

She could see that the Russian General was gazing at her with undisguised astonishment.

Before anyone could say anything Latasha asked,

"Do you speak English, General?"

The General shook his head.

"Then I will explain to you in your language," she said in Russian, "that I am here because it is the suggestion of Her Imperial Majesty, Queen Victoria of Great Britain that I should marry His Royal Highness Prince Kraus of Oldessa."

She turned to smile at Prince Kraus, as she added,

"However, we both wished to keep our engagement a secret until I discovered a little more about this beautiful country over which the Prince reigns.

"So I have not stayed here under my real name and we intended to keep Her Majesty's project secret until my brother, the Duke, arrives in two or three days.

"With him will be a representative of Her Majesty Queen Victoria and he will be present when our marriage is solemnised."

Then in a thick and harsh voice the Russian General demanded,

"Can you prove who you are, madam?"

"But of course I can. Here is my passport on which you will see, as you have just heard, that I am the sister of the Duke of Norlington."

She held out her passport.

As the General took it, she held up the book which was in her hand.

"*This*," she proclaimed, "is the family tree of the Norlingtons and you will see quite clearly that my mother, Princess Beatrice, was a cousin of Francis Ferdinand, Duke of Saxe-Coburg the uncle of Her Majesty Queen Victoria."

The Russian General was defeated and he knew it.

He made no attempt to look at the book, but handed Latasha back her passport.

Then with more dignity than Latasha expected, he bowed to her and Prince Kraus.

140

"I see, Your Royal Highness," he said, speaking the language of Oldessa in a somewhat faulty way, "there has been some small misunderstanding. I can only apologise and wish Your Royal Highness every happiness."

"I think that my people will be very happy," Prince Kraus replied, "when they can fly the Union Jack beside our own flag. And I am most fortunate in having the most beautiful wife in the whole of the Balkans!"

The General did not answer him, but merely bowed stiffly again.

Turning round he marched from the Throne Room followed by the Officers who had accompanied him.

Everyone recognised that he must be seen off the premises formally, so the Lord Chamberlain hurried after the Russians followed by several *aides-de-camp*.

There was an audible sigh of relief from the Prime Minister and the Members of the Oldessan Cabinet.

Then the Prime Minister walked forward to stretch out his hand to Prince Kraus.

"I have the singular honour of wishing Your Royal Highness every happiness," he announced, "and this news will delight our people, who will, for the first time in several years, sleep soundly in their beds without being afraid."

"I am well aware of that," said Prince Kraus. "I can only say God has been very merciful and as Lady Latasha has told you our marriage will take place just as soon as her brother, the Duke of Norlington, arrives and with him whoever will represent Her Majesty Queen Victoria."

"The people of Oldessa will be thrilled when I tell them the news," added the Prime Minister. "I am going to issue the order now that every Church bell in the country rings a peal of joy and thankfulness that we are saved from the evil grasp of the Russians!"

He bowed to Prince Kraus and next to Latasha.

Then he walked to the door followed by the rest of his entourage.

As the last man left, obviously in a hurry to make sure the Russians had really gone, Prince Kraus spoke to the remaining *aides-de-camp* and they left too.

They closed the door behind them and Latasha then realised that she was alone in the Throne Room with Prince Kraus.

She had not dared to look at him while everything was taking place.

Now she was surprised to see an expression in his eyes that she did not understand.

For a moment there was complete silence between them.

Then Prince Kraus blurted out almost angrily,

"How could you have let me suffer all the fires of hell, because I thought I could never marry you?"

As he spoke he put out his arms and pulled her, not gently but roughly, against him.

Then he was kissing her.

Kissing her wildly as if he had been terrified that he might have lost her.

Latasha had never been kissed before.

She thought for a moment it was a different feeling from what she had expected.

Then she felt the magical ecstasy she had felt when she realised that she was in love with him.

It swept over her whole body.

It was so much more wonderful and more perfect than anything she had dreamt about.

'I love you! I love you!' she wanted to scream as he drew her closer and still closer.

He kissed her fiercely as if he just could no longer control himself.

It was quite impossible for her to think, only to feel a wonder and a glory that carried Latasha up into the sky.

After what seemed to her a very long time he raised his head.

"My darling, you have driven me almost mad," he sighed. "Even now I can hardly believe you are real and I will not wake up to find this is a wonderful dream."

"I just had to save you from the Russians," Latasha murmured.

"Why did you not tell me before?" he demanded.

For a moment Latasha hesitated.

Then she said,

"I did not think you loved me and because I loved you so much, I thought it would be an unbearable agony if you married me only because I was Royal."

Prince Kraus gave a strangled laugh.

"I fell in love with you from the first moment I saw you, and I knew after you had massaged my forehead that what I felt for you was different from anything I had ever known."

"You love me, you really love me?" Latasha asked breathlessly.

"I have been going nearly crazy, trying to work out some way of forcing Stefan to take a Royal bride, so then I could marry *you*."

Latasha stared at him.

"I don't – understand."

"It was the only way I could ever make you mine, my dearest darling. I have already written to Harry telling him to bring his sister Latasha here immediately. I thought that if she is as attractive as she was as a child, Stefan, who is always captivated by a new face, would undoubtedly fall in love with her. Then he could take over the country and I could marry you!"

Latasha looked at him in astonishment.

"You were prepared to give up Oldessa for *me*?"

"I would give up the whole world rather than lose you. I knew it was impossible to go on living without you. Thus it was the only solution I could find to the dreadful problem of how Oldessa would be able to wave the Union Jack and stay independent."

Latasha sighed.

Then as he drew her close again, she asked him,

"How could I have possibly known? How could I have guessed that you loved me? I was so unhappy last night thinking that while I loved you with all my heart, you would never feel the same about me."

"I love you more than I can *ever* put into words, my Latasha. I am going to spend the rest of my life making love to you, so that you will understand just what I feel for you."

"Harry will have to tell the Queen that we are to be married. I expect that she will be annoyed that she did not think of us first!"

"It does not matter who thought about it or who did not. All that matters is you will be my wife and as quickly as possible. I am now going to send your brother a cable, and you shall help me word it, so that he understands we are patiently waiting for his arrival and the finest horses in my Kingdom are at his disposal."

Latasha laughed.

"It will certainly bring Harry here swiftly if nothing else does!"

Then she gave a cry.

"You promised me you would rest before luncheon. Instead of which you have been worried by the Russians. We must go at once and tell Nanny and Amalie that they have gone. When I left them they were terrified."

"I was terrified too," he admitted. "And when you swept in, I could not believe that what I was hearing was true."

Latasha put her head on his shoulder.

"I had only just told Nanny that we are going home tomorrow, because I really believed that what you would suggest to me this afternoon might be something totally different."

"How could you underestimate me and my love so completely?"

"You never showed me in any way that you loved me," murmured Latasha.

"If I had touched you, I would have taken you into my arms and kissed you, as I am going to kiss you again now. But I had to think of a way of saving Oldessa and at the same time not losing you. That was something I knew I could never face. If you left me, I had no wish to go on living."

There was a note of sincerity in his voice that was very moving.

Then Latasha gently suggested,

"Come and let's have luncheon now. Then I insist on you resting afterwards."

"Only if you rest with me, my darling, and we will plan our wedding. I know that everyone in the country will dance with such joy that we need no longer be afraid of the Russians. And they will be as thrilled as I am at having such a beautiful Princess to rule over them."

"It all sounds so very exciting, but you are to come and sit down and eat your luncheon. Then I am going to massage your head so that you will go to sleep."

"I refuse to sleep when I can be talking to you, my darling Latasha."

"Until I become your wife I intend to be your nurse. Therefore you will have to do what I say."

"We will soon see about that! I worship and adore you, my Latasha, but I still intend to be Master in my own house."

He kissed her tenderly and then they walked arm in arm towards the closed door.

When the door opened, they could see almost every inhabitant in the Palace was gathered there.

A great cheer rang out.

The next moment Prince Kraus and Latasha were covered with flower petals.

After luncheon was finished and they were talking quietly in his room, an *aide-de-camp* came in.

"Forgive me bothering Your Royal Highness," he said, "but there is a huge crowd outside the Palace calling for you and the Lord Chamberlain thinks that Your Royal Highness should make an appearance."

Prince Kraus laughed.

"The story has already reached the City!"

Latasha quickly tidied up her hair which had been disarranged by his kisses.

Then they walked upstairs to the first floor window of the Palace.

When the enormous crowd gathering beneath saw them, they went mad and the cheers were deafening.

Hats, handkerchiefs and anything else to hand were flung into the air.

Latasha and Prince Kraus waved in reply until their arms ached.

After twenty minutes they were back in the Palace, but they were obliged to appear four more times before the crowd gradually and happily dispersed.

*

The wedding of His Royal Highness Prince Kraus of Oldessa and Lady Latasha Ling of Great Britain was the most spectacular and glamorous event that had ever taken place in any country of the Balkans.

Latasha was given away by her brother, the Duke of Norlington.

A very overexcited Princess Amalie was the Chief Bridesmaid. She was followed by ten small bridesmaids from the most distinguished families in the country.

Every Church in Oldessa was splendidly decorated in cascades of flowers as well as the great City Cathedral where Latasha and Prince Kraus were married.

Huge throngs of citizens crowded the streets of the City.

The Archbishop of Oldessa performed the marriage and Latasha found the Service deeply moving.

After she became Prince Kraus's wife, he crowned her with an ancient golden crown that had been worn by every Oldessan Princess for many centuries.

She could see by the love in his eyes how much it all meant to him.

'I will always love him and look after him until we both die,' Latasha vowed silently.

When the wedding was over, dancing and singing went on all night.

The British Secretary of State for Foreign Affairs, the Marquis of Salisbury, had arrived promptly with the Duke to represent Queen Victoria.

He brought with him a present from Her Majesty and a letter in her own hand wishing them every happiness and peace in their country for the rest of their lives.

Latasha thought that there were almost more Union Jacks to be seen than the striped yellow and green flag of Oldessa.

The flowers that were thrown into the open carriage in which they were driven away from the Cathedral almost enveloped them in petals of every colour.

It was not only a brilliantly happy occasion for the people of Oldessa.

It was also a formidable warning to the Russians to stop intimidating the Balkans and stay away.

Latasha had discovered something most important in the few days before she was married.

It was that now he was well again Prince Kraus had every intention of making his country a model to all his neighbours.

And that in future Oldessans would be extremely prosperous went without saying.

Latasha recognised that the people themselves were happy and that they had almost everything they required was an example to other Principalities.

Some of the Balkan States were not as fortunate in their Ruler and they were not fully exploiting all that was waiting to be discovered in their mountains, their cascading rivers and in the soil itself.

"I have very big plans for Oldessa. I always have had," Prince Kraus said to Latasha. "And now, my darling, since I have you, it is going to be very much easier than it would have been."

"I do so want to help you, my Prince, and it will be wonderful if we can work together," sighed Latasha.

"After tomorrow," he had said the night before the wedding, "we will not be two people but one and I have no use for my throne if you do not sit beside me."

It was thrilling for Latasha to realise that she had found a man who appreciated not only her looks, but also her brain.

Prince Kraus had already asked her for her advice on everything he was planning.

Latasha was intelligent and she knew that anything she suggested was exactly what he wanted to hear.

When the Duke arrived he was delighted to find his sister was so happy – and that his friend Kraus was riding as well as he ever did.

"If it had not been for your sister," Prince Kraus told him, "I do not think I would ever have been able to mount a horse again."

"That would have been a major disaster," the Duke had replied, "especially as your horses are so outstanding. But what am I to give you as a wedding present?"

"You are giving me the greatest happiness anyone could ask for in this world, Harry, but I thought it would be rather amusing if you entered some of your horses from England in a race held on our Racecourse."

The Duke looked surprised.

"It will help to make it an international affair," he explained, "and not confined entirely to Oldessa."

"That is an excellent idea!" the Duke exclaimed.

"It will unite a great number of Principalities," he continued, "and if they are friendly with each other, it will make it more difficult for the Czar to force them under Russian rule."

"Of course it will, Kraus, and nothing brings men of different nationalities together better than horses."

"That is exactly what I feel as well, Harry, and of course we will have support from Austria and Hungary."

"We used to dream of something like this when we were at Oxford," the Duke now remarked, "but somehow I could never think of you running an international Race-course!"

"That is what I intend to have among a great many other projects here in Oldessa and I am sure long before the Racecourse is finished Latasha will have a thousand other ideas which I will want to put into operation."

The Duke put his hand on Prince Kraus's shoulder.

"I cannot think of anyone I would rather have as a brother-in-law than you, Kraus, and it seems almost as if this was planned from the moment we met."

"God has been so very good to me, Harry, and as Latasha saved my life, it is now hers for ever."

*

It was something he repeated to Latasha the night after they were married.

She had been rather surprised that Prince Kraus had been so determined to be married in the morning.

"Weddings usually take place in the afternoon," she had pointed out.

"We are going to be different," he replied. "We are to be married in the morning. The people we will entertain will insist on speeches at an early luncheon that will take place immediately afterwards in the Palace."

"Then what happens?" asked Latasha.

"We will go away on our honeymoon."

She smiled at him.

"I have not yet asked where we are going."

"I have not told you, because it is to be a secret and a surprise."

"But I have to know," she protested. "If you do not tell me, I will not know what clothes to wear."

She spoke without thinking and then as she saw the smile on his face, she blushed.

"I adore you when you blush. Oh my darling one, I have so many things to teach you about love and it is going to take me a long time."

"We will start with my lessons on our honeymoon," she said. "That is why I want to know where it will be?"

She thought as she asked the question that she did not particularly want to go anywhere in France.

The memory of the Comte was still lurking in her consciousness.

But even if they spent their honeymoon together at a nice quiet resort, people would stare at them.

There had been so much written in the newspapers about their wedding and the dramatic story of how she had saved Prince Kraus's life and how he had not known who she really was until his country was threatened by hordes of Russians.

The story had lost nothing in the telling.

Everyone thought that it was the most romantic and exciting tale they had ever heard.

Latasha felt that it was wonderful that everything had ended so happily.

But at the same time it would be a bore if on their honeymoon, they were pursued by people congratulating them and talking too much.

"If you insist," Prince Kraus was saying, "I will tell you where I am taking you."

"I am listening most attentively – "

"Several years ago when I wanted to study some

particular subject and was tired of Court protocol, I built myself a tiny house halfway up one of our mountains."

"A house!" exclaimed Latasha.

"It is very small but very comfortable and I used to go there for two or three days at a time when I wanted to be alone to have time to think."

He paused for a moment.

"I have never taken anyone to the house with me and I realise now that I was waiting for you, my darling, and our honeymoon."

Latasha drew in her breath.

"It sounds fascinating, Kraus."

"It is, and I have a dear old couple to look after me. She is a brilliant cook and he was at one time my father's valet. They are perfectly happy living in my little hide-away in the mountains and they will both be so thrilled to look after us."

"And we are going there alone?"

"Entirely alone and that, my darling, is when I will teach you about love and punish you with so many kisses for making me so desperately unhappy when I was afraid I must lose either you or my country!"

"But now you have both," cried Latasha. "So you cannot be greedy about anything else."

He smiled tenderly at her.

Without saying anything she knew he was thinking that one day she would give him an heir – a son to carry on with the plans he was making for his country.

The colour rose brightly in her cheeks and Prince Kraus laughed quietly.

"You see, my darling, I can read your thoughts as you can read mine. That is another reason which makes it impossible for us to be apart from each other. It makes us sure that we are one person and it is how we will remain together from now until Eternity."

*

"I love you, my Kraus," Latasha whispered to him some days later.

They were crossing the threshold of the little house in the mountains.

It was exactly like an enchanted cottage in a fairy tale and the view was breathtaking.

"And I love you," he answered. "With all my heart, all my soul and, my darling, with my body and my brain."

They were the first words they said to each other as they entered the house.

Latasha thought that they would remember them for ever.

Then Prince Kraus took her across the room to a window which overlooked the valley below.

Far away on the horizon they could see the roof of the Royal Palace in the City.

"Now we are like a God and Goddess looking down from the Heavens on all our people beneath us," he said quietly. "They are our people and we have today dedicated ourselves to their service.

Latasha put her head against his shoulder.

"I know, because our love is so great," he went on, "that it will make not only the people of our country happy, but spread further and further so that our Oldessa will be a magic word to help others less fortunate."

Latasha gave a little cry.

"Oh, my darling, only you could think of anything so wonderful. It is just what I want you to think and what I want you to feel."

"It is what you make me think and feel, Latasha. All the beautiful and ambitious ideas which come into my mind now come from you and are part of you just as they are part of me. That, my darling one, is what we, from our perfect little Heaven, are going to give the world beneath us."

Then he was kissing her.

Kissing her demandingly and passionately.

As they clung together, Latasha believed that God had answered all her prayers and she had found love.

The true real love she had always believed existed if only she could find it.

Now she would never lose that perfect love.

'I love you, I adore you,' she tried to say.

But there was no need for words.

The love they felt swept them up into the sky.

They were no longer human.

They were part of God who is Love and who takes those who find it into an Eternity of happiness.